Totally Bound Publishing books by Amber Malloy

Spies R Us
Spies R Us
Kill Shot

Perfect Stats
Winning Her
Hard Knox
Hawk

Perfect Stats

HAWK

AMBER MALLOY

Hawk
ISBN # 978-1-83943-727-4
©Copyright Amber Malloy 2021
Cover Art by Louisa Maggio ©Copyright August 2021
Interior text design by Claire Siemaszkiewicz
Totally Bound Publishing

HAWK

Dedication

To my child prodigy motorcycle-riding gremlin of
an old man.
Thanks, Dad.

Prologue

June

Stepping into the dimly lit dive, Hawthorn Maze, aka Hawk, propped open the door to his favorite dingy blues bar and hoisted the Keating Cup above his head. Greeted by a wave of cheers, he took that moment to soak up his well-deserved glory.

Ten years ago, the Chicago Northern Royals had been the team to beat. In the span of a decade, the hockey darlings had bashed their way through the earth's crust and straight to its inner core. Career-ending injuries, along with drugs and the occasional sex scandals, had plagued them. The champions had no longer been considered a threat. They had become merely the butt of a joke on late-night talk shows.

Hawk had taken a huge leap of faith joining the crew of misfits. More than once he'd wanted to cut his losses and retire, but after three long years, he'd finally gotten what he wanted…no, desired. The Royals had entered the playoffs as underdogs and left championship winners.

Downright fanatical about their sports teams to a psychotic degree, the city of Chicago celebrated the win with a loony fever. Everyone, even the mayor, was left with a major sports hangover.

For one whole day, the first-string players were allowed to take the trophy home. Unfortunately, his teammates hadn't gotten the memo that explicitly excluded them from attending his day with the award. Five of the Northern Royal rookies sat in the booth taking selfies and ussies. Since kicking them out would look bad, he chucked the trophy on top of his right shoulder and made his way around the bar.

Raised in Ontario, Canada's foster system, Hawk had picked Moe's Blues Bar to celebrate his 'trophy day' and invited all the people he loved for support.

Moe's was a hole in the wall that never got too much foot traffic. That's why he'd initially fallen in love with the dump in the first place. He considered the blues bar his home away from home.

Hawk hadn't even told the press where he would spend his day with the Keating Cup. However, a few reporters waited for him in the back. He could probably thank his teammates for that shit.

"Congrats, Hawk." Simone, the light-skinned bartender with the crazy-cool one-sided mohawk, reached across the bar to slap his hand.

"Where's Moe?" He asked after the blues legend and bar owner, Sugarfoot Mosely — the father figure in his surrogate family.

"A little under the weather. He sends his apologies and wants me to give the whole bar a round."

"Cool, just make sure my teammates over there are long gone when that happens."

Simone threw him a wink and turned back to pouring the beers on tap.

Accepting his much-earned accolades from the regulars, Hawk headed over to the booths. He shook a few patrons' hands before he stopped in front of his teammates.

He patiently waited for the fans who surrounded the young'uns to thin out before he broadened the grin on his face. Leaning closer to the obnoxious interlopers, he stopped himself from choking the little shits.

"What's up, assholes? Why are you here?" He barely wanted to see them during the season. The idiots wanted all the shine without any of the sweat it took to win. Hawk had to deal with them half of the year. The other six months were all his.

"We didn't want you to look pathetic," the youngest and most obnoxious of the bunch said. Baby-faced brats, mostly from Sweden and Canada, stupidly stared back at him.

"No family and no first string… The press will dub you Little Orphan Annie."

The group of degenerates drunkenly laughed at his family-less status.

"Well, I didn't invite the paps, much less you fucks, sooo see your way out."

"Come on," Swedish meatball number two said. "We'll take a couple of pics then go off to a real bar."

"Yeah, this one is full of old people — and it sucks." Smug as hell, the rookies actually thought they could poach his moment.

"Hawk!" The bar went wild, which meant the people he'd actually invited had arrived.

"Sorry we're late… Traffic."

Hawk turned away from the moment stealers to slap hands with Gavin Knox, his childhood best friend.

Along with him came Andre, their college bud and all-around asshole extraordinaire, plus their families, to celebrate his championship win.

"Ah shit, it's the football players," the Northern Royals defenseman snorted. "The has-beens."

"Did a bench warmer just insult me?" Andre Burnett, former running back for the Mavericks, stepped forward.

"Oh, hey, you just admitted to watching the game." Hawk laughed at the former running back's slip-up. Disgusted that a half-black man would pick such a girly sport, Andre never missed a chance to poke fun at hockey.

"Hell, I don't watch that shit! Look at them." Andre snorted. "You can tell they don't see any action."

"Do you want a taste of this, old man?" The rookie scrunched up his face with a baby cub growl.

Andre folded back the sleeves of his dress shirt. "Come on, Macaulay Culkin. Let's cash that check your ass can't write."

"Ignore them." Hawk waved the press over. "They were just leaving." He waited for the little jerks to scoot out of the booth.

"You're missing a prime opportunity to increase your followers, dude," Sweden muttered on his way past.

"In football, the kiddies knew their place," Andre stated.

"That is a blatant lie." Knox disputed Andre's claim.

"Everyone get close and shut up," Hawk demanded.

As the press crowded around their mosh-posh little gang, he hopped into the center. Knox moved to his right with his two toddlers and his wife, while Andre's brood of five flanked his left side.

"On the count of four." Since all of them were pros at the media game, everyone plastered smiles on their faces.

"One…two…three… Champions!" they screamed.

Chapter One

As Lexi Waters' advanced coding class put the finishing touches on their latest assignment, she flew her fingers across the screen of her phone a million miles per hour. Drowning out the *click clack* sound from more than a dozen girls pounding away on their keyboards, she polished off her last text.

"Okay, girls!" she hollered over the noise while pushing away from her desk. "We've got fifteen minutes left, but I wanted to say…uh—" Flashing lights drew her attention toward the window. A police cruiser turned into the community center's parking lot. *Shit!* Standing up, she slid her phone into the back pocket of her jeans before she stepped in front of her students.

"Girls, code has been one of the biggest joys in my life, and you guys will never know how much you truly mean to me…" Lexi took in each one of the girls' faces, wanting to commit every detail to memory. "I'll be taking a little time away, which means I won't be able to teach the class." Groans filled the room at her announcement. Lexi had been with some of these girls since their tween years.

Do not cry. Do not cry. Swallowing the emerging lump in her throat, she encouraged herself to keep it together for a smidge longer.

"Miss Tracy will be taking over for the foreseeable future." Lexi steadily ignored her phone buzzing in her back pocket. "She will help you tie up the loose ends on your video game concepts, starting with the plot all the way down to character development."

"But we wanted to do it with you," the best coder in the group whined.

"Uh, don't worry," Lexi's assistant Tracy groused. "I'm not standing here or anything."

Limited on time, Lexi refused to acknowledge the little feud that had been brewing between them for weeks.

"Trust me. You guys are in good hands. You're all set for the Fire Code submissions, and... Well" — she took a deep breath because goodbyes were always hard — "every single one of you is intelligent, awesome and there's nothing you can't and won't do. Now make me proud!" She pounded her fist in the air with more enthusiasm than she actually felt.

Chairs scraped against the tile floor, the sounds bouncing off the concrete walls as the girls unexpectedly rushed her. Lexi stumbled back from the weight of their enormous group hug. For a moment, she allowed herself to open up, and lowering her head on top of her students, she soaked up all the good feels.

"Ms. Lexi." The smallest in the class reached up and pulled something out of the messy bun piled on top of her head. "You have glass in your hair."

"Oh?" She took the chunk out of the girl's hand. "Mirror broke." With assistance from her soon-to-be-ex-husband's golf club — she had smashed it into a million pieces. She was snatched out of the warm comfort of her hugs when the community center secretary waved from the small window in the door. "Okay, time to go. Take care, girls."

Determined to not get emotional, Lexi slipped away from the girls' surprisingly strong grips. Grabbing the doorknob to open the door, she turned back to wave goodbye, leaving her home away from home.

"Ms. Stewart—"

"Waters," Lexi corrected the nervous woman. She needed to distance herself from her ex-husband's name ASAP.

"The community center's director doesn't understand…"

Flinging the piece of mirror into the janitor's cart on her way past, Lexi tuned the woman out. Josh had always loved her hair long, but the weight of her curls had grown into a burden. Lexi couldn't wait to change it. She had narrowed down the haircut she wanted to either a symmetrical chic or a perfect Toni Braxton à la *Betty Boop* pixie cut.

"Ms. Stewart!" a couple of boys on the basketball court yelled.

She waved at the teens, fighting off the mist in her eyes. The kids were about the only thing she wished she could take with her.

"I'm sorry. What did you say?"

"The officers wouldn't tell me what they wanted to talk to you about," she nervously babbled, "but I put them near the back door like you suggested."

"Did you get the numbers that I sent you?"

As they walked through the corridors of the enormous Inglewood Center, the secretary fumbled with her phone. It took every ounce of Lexi's patience not to snatch it from her hands. "Moe's Blues and Jazz,

Sugarfoot Moe Waters and or Simone, the manager of the club, correct?"

"Yes, perfect," Lexi told her.

"And forgive me for being obtuse, but why did you send me these numbers?"

"Bail money." She walked into the administrator's front office. Thankfully, there was an exit away from the classroom, where none of the kids could witness their mentor's arrest. #*superembarrassing*. "If you would be so kind as to call them and let them know that I will need to be bailed out, that would be awesome."

"Excuse me?"

"The asshole I will soon be divorced from froze all my assets." She shrugged. "So, yeah, there's that."

"Lexington Stewart?" Two officers waited for her.

"Waters," she corrected the cop. All she'd done was smash every breakable item in Josh's secret hideaway. Considering it was her hard work that had paid for that crap, it technically shouldn't have been a jail-able offense.

"Lexington Waters, you have the right to remain silent." The stocky officer who demonstrated a severe case of Napoleon complex grabbed her arm a little too harshly and handcuffed her.

For a minute, it crossed her mind to feign innocence, but she was super guilty, because…

Fuck Josh. That's why!

* * * *

July

Mold. The courthouse actually smelled worse than fungus, but Lexi had finally put her finger on the suffocating stench.

Avoiding eye contact with the bailiff, she waited for him to relieve her of the intrusive ankle monitor she had named 'Roach'. No one liked a roach unless a joint was on the other end of it. The device was listed in the 'wouldn't miss' category she had made, a lot like the state of California or her ex-husband. In less than two hours she would be on a plane to Chicago, two thousand and fifteen miles away from the mess that had become her life.

"Good to go, ma'am. I bet you're happy to get that off." Lexi had intentionally worn high heels and a skirt for this celebratory moment. Feeling lighter but not necessarily better, she eyed the bailiff without allowing him any indication that she needed to chat. He may have wanted to extend a bit of levity to a crap situation, but chit-chat was never her thing.

"Ms. Stewart." She lifted her eyes away from the angry welt the monitor had made and toward her attorney.

"Waters... The last name is Waters." Lexi bent over to rub her ankle.

"Let's go over the terms of your probation," Maureen Wendt said.

"Uh, didn't we already do that?" she asked her no-nonsense lawyer.

"Yes, but I want to make sure you fully understand."

At the age of twenty, Lexi had built her own company from the ground up. Of course, everyone thought Josh was the man behind the firm and not her because *Fuck Josh. That's why!* Before SugarTech had made major strides, *Wired Magazine* had declared it the most promising firm since Macintosh.

Fast forward to twelve years later and her ex-husband had decided to snatch the rug out from under her...literally. The fucker even took her rug.

Wanting to get the whole thing over with, she nodded.

"A distance of one hundred yards must be maintained between you and the company's campus."

"Never went there anyway," Lexi mumbled.

Maureen shot her a glare before she continued. "Effective immediately, you must vacate your position in the company. Your seat on the board will be in question until a judgment has been rendered on the charges that were levied against you."

"Hold on. I thought my criminal charges were dropped." Lexi ran her hand across her fresh pixie cut. In ye olde tradition of pissed bitch, she had whacked most of her hair off.

"That was for the case with your ex-husband. Remember that the board members have levied their own criminal charges and a civil suit against you." Maureen heaved a considerably frustrated sigh in her direction. "We're still working to get those charges dismissed." She checked her phone as she continued to reel off a long list of transgressions. "Until then, the conditions of your bail will have to stay in place."

Grabbing her purse, Lexi stood. Maureen was seriously testing the boundaries of the little bit of patience she had left.

"This may not be the outcome we hoped for, but it's the best we're going to get under the circumstances. Perhaps next time you'll control your temper and not break into your ex's house to childishly destroy all his belongings."

"Considering it was my money, I technically destroyed my own shit."

"According to California law —"

In the past, she'd been accused of not expressing herself very well. Since her world had been flipped upside down, Lexi had communicated her emotions a tad differently. She pushed open the revolving door and stepped away from Maureen mid-sentence, leaving the lawyer — and soon California — behind her.

Chapter Two

Two months later

Banished from California and anything involving technology, Lexi stood in the middle of Moe's Blues and Jazz bar. Mesmerized by the NASDAQ ticker at the bottom of the overhead television screen, she forgot about her surroundings. More enthralled with the fresh-faced singer who performed Nina Simone's *Don't Let Me Be Misunderstood* on the tiny stage than her little trance, Moe's patrons ignored her.

"Boss lady!" Simone, the bartender, waved her hand wide across the busy bar, snapping Lexi out of her haze. "Table three." She slid the tray across the bar. Since they were a couple of waitresses short, Lexi had volunteered to pitch in for the night.

Grabbing the drinks, she maneuvered her way the packed room. The NASDAQ numbers went through her mind. Anything she created under the umbrella of SugarTech had been put on indefinite hold — which meant there was no way the company had time to roll out anything that could produce that type of jump in stock numbers.

Lexi stopped at the table of suits, who were probably scouts from one of the music labels.

"Talk to me, cutie?" one of the guys pressed. Ever since she'd renovated the dusty interior of Moe's and added younger talent to the roster, the sharks in the water hunted for fresh blood. "Do you break the law often? Because I'd give you a speeding ticket for getting this heart of mine racing."

She set their drinks down in front of them. "Well, I've never got a speeding ticket before, but if you want to charge me with assault..." Lexi scrunched up her face before throwing them a lazy shrug. "Holler if you need anything, fellas."

As soon as she turned away from the buttoned-up trolls, Lexi's mind went back to the end-of-day market. Until all ligations against her were settled, nothing with her name could be introduced into the public sector. Deep in the muck of her own thoughts, she slid up to the bar and waited for her next order.

"Can I offer you some friendly advice?" Simone cooed, while batting her purple-colored eyelashes at her. "Hire more servers."

"But that was funny," Lexi defended herself. "You told me to be funny."

As she continued to pour the beer on tap, Simone threw a weary glance over her shoulder.

"Sorry," Lexi apologized. Not used to uncomfortable shoes, she switched from one high-heel-covered foot to another. "I've been looking." Attempting to ignore the pulsating pain in her arches, she waited for Simone to complete her next order. She didn't think she'd be on her feet all day serving beers to blues lovers...*cough, cough,* posers.

Her father had wanted to help with her mounting legal bills and felt her tech background could be useful. She didn't have the heart to tell him that coding and business weren't exactly peanut butter and jelly.

"Not to mention that I can't seem to find anyone more awesome than you," Lexi cooed.

"Slick." Simone, the tattoo-covered sweetheart, frowned. "Seriously, if you want to keep up this good flow, you better get new employees in here — and quick."

Lexi probably should have kept a couple of people on staff, but she couldn't overlook the missing toilet rolls or the occasional whisky bottle that grew legs and walked straight out of the door. If they weren't garbage people who basically sucked, she would have kept them on for a little while longer.

"Trust me, girl. This cool-ass renovation job will all be for nothing if no one serves these people," Simone said.

"Oh, so this is *your* fault," a deep voice grumbled.

Lexi's gaze went up the skyscraper that led to a solid wall of bulging muscle. Once she made it to the peak of the mountain, an incredibly pissed-off bronze man received all her attention.

Confused by the life-sized *Mortal Kombat* character in front of her, she slid the bartender a wide-eyed stare. "Hawk here works from time to time," Simone rushed to explain.

"Everyone had to reapply for their position," Lexi told him. "If you don't mind doing a background check, Simone can get... Ah, Hawk was it?" She wondered if it was hopefully short for something else. "She'll get you an application to fill out."

"Are you serious?"

"Oh shit," Simone muttered before she zipped her way to the opposite end of the bar.

"Like I said, everyone had to do it." Why the hell was he mad? She hadn't even fired him. Lexi would have remembered a dude this chiseled... Crap, she meant big. Nevertheless, her mind was on constant pinball tilt. It was hard to keep track of all the everyday changes she had recently undergone. There was no way a misplaced extra from *Conan the Barbarian* would have slipped through the broken cracks of her mind — or *could* he? "Well, Simone and Peaches didn't have to, but they were the only two not smuggling contraband up their *culo*, sooo..."

The giant lowered his eyelids to tiny slits, which was a shame because his smoldering hazel eyes were beyond sexy. *What the hell is that?* she silently checked herself.

"Where's Moe?" he growled.

"Un-avail-able." She spoke slowly to the man-child who towered over her.

"Simone," he hollered, staring daggers into her soul, "where's Moe?"

"At home!"

"Did you just pull a 'let me speak to your manager'?" she asked, blown away by the balls on this one.

"Cool." Hawk turned away from her, and with the sheer force of his presence moved the crowd out of his path.

Cataloging one of the stranger encounters she had since moving to Chicago, Lexi grabbed the empty bottles on top of the bar and threw them in the trash.

Even the thieving-ass dishwasher who had tried to walk out of the door with three pounds of buffalo wings in his pants rated less awkward than her Hawk experience. Of course, it didn't help that the sexy ogre smelled expensively delicious. The undeniable scent of cedar, spice and, if she was not mistaken, freaking violets lingered long after he had walked out of the door.

What the hell did the big dude steal to afford cologne worth over four hundred dollars? The fragrance had taken her back to her not-so-distant tech-loving past.

The aromatic reminder of her current predicament had Lexi fighting off the urge to unload a feral scream. A fierce type of yell that usually erupted from the belly was clawing its way out of her lungs to explode from her throat. Having to abandon the company she'd built from the ground up was a bitter pill to swallow — and for what? To serve a room full of corporate assholes drinks.

"Lexi, table five," Simone called out, interrupting her mini breakdown.

"Got it!" she screamed back, unleashing a little bit of the buildup trapped inside her. Stacking the mugs of beer on her tray, she beat back the urge to fall into a crying heap across the floor.

* * * *

It took over twelve city blocks for Hawk to cool down. He had blown past his anger around block five and settled into mildly annoyed once he got closer to the Mavericks' front office. As he jogged across the busy street to the stadium, a car screeched inches away from him.

"Whoa!" he yelled, slapping the hood of the taxi.

"Big man!" The driver poked his head out of the open window. "Got time for a selfie?"

Happy he didn't have to beat the driver to a bloody pulp, Hawk relaxed his stance. "Sure."

"Come on, dude. Hurry up! I have a plane to catch," his passenger complained from the back seat. Hawk went to the driver's side and ducked his head in the front window.

"Don't be disrespectful," the cabbie threw over his shoulder before he smiled and took the picture. "Thanks, my man. The fam will go crazy when they see this. We don't have too many of you around, if you get my meaning."

"Can we go now?" the passenger whined.

Hawk stepped away from the cab with a chuckle and trotted toward the stadium door.

"It's O'Hare," the driver grunted. "Your plane won't be leaving on time."

The automatic doors to the Mavericks' football team's executive office building slid open. Hawk stepped inside. All partied out from his hockey teams' championship win, he'd taken over a month off. The second that his contractual obligations ended, he'd pointed his Harley north and ridden to his hometown of Ontario, Canada. For one straight month he'd traveled through North America on his hog.

"Silver Surfer!" the security staffer shouted.

He waved on his way past. Thanks to his relationship with all the team's higher-ups, everyone recognized him. A sport star in his own right, Hawk realized early on that just because football and hockey weren't exactly the recipe for Reese's Pieces candy, they didn't necessarily taste great together. "Your guy got a new office, top floor."

"No shit." Envious of the cushy life his best friend had carved out for himself, Hawk waited for the guard to call for the executive elevator. When the doors slid apart, he stepped into the cab and tried to tamp down his shitty mood.

Toward the beginning of his career, he'd made every rookie mistake in the book. Around his second season and first trade, the coaches had sat him down and told him he was officially out of chances. If he didn't turn his life around, they would get rid of him mid-season — no ifs, ands or buts about it.

For eight whole years he hadn't partied or touched a drink. Unfortunately, the press had never let him forget his drunken exploits or shitty soundbites from his early twenties.

He even had to stop his 'hit it and quit it' groupie love. Needless to say, the no-strings-attached sex was harder to let go than the drinking. Moe's bar had helped keep him out of trouble. No one but old-timers and blues-lovers hung out there. The customers didn't give a shit about his career or treat him any differently, so the place had become a home away from home.

Unfortunately, the renovation had turned the bar into a shiny shell of its former self, and it rubbed him the wrong way.

As the elevator doors opened, Hawk stepped onto the executive floor.

"Mr. Maze." The young assistant smirked.

"Lucy." He nodded. "I could have sworn I told you to call me Hawk."

"That seems unprofessional." A pink flush crept up her neck. "And since my boss told me to stay far, far away from you…"

"How about we split the difference and you call me Mr. Hawk?"

The receptionist shyly tucked her hair behind her ear and nodded. "Okay, *Mr.* Hawk."

Hawk winked at her while he pointed at Knox's office — "Can I?" — and grabbed the doorknob.

"Yes, he's waiting for you."

The secretary's giggles followed him in.

"Stop flirting with my employees," his best friend greeted him. Gavin Knox stood behind his desk, passing a sippy cup to one of the two cutest kids Hawk had ever laid eyes on.

"Unc Hawwwwk!" the other screamed. She pushed herself up onto her chubby baby legs near her father's desk. Bending down, he caught the bundle of pink frilliness who ran straight at him. As she hugged him tight, he kissed the curly-haired little cherub's head.

"What is this, take your kids to work day? Where's your cooler, hotter half?" Hawk stood up with the baby tightly gripping his neck.

"MIA. She dropped off the kids then chucked me deuces." Knox bounced the baby up and down before he scooped his cell phone off his desk. "How was your trip?"

"Peaceful, meditative and very, very calming."

Amazingly, Knox managed to text with his left hand while cradling the almost two-year-old toddler with his right. "Sounds boring as F."

Hawk stared into the face of what could have been the perfect All-American quarterback — except he wasn't. The former four-peat Mega Bowl winner who had graced every sports cover, cereal box and TV screen was one hundred percent pure Canadian.

The perfect specimen of a sports hero, Knox had pivoted careers seamlessly. He'd gone from everyone's favorite quarterback to overseer of the number one football team in the United States. "Sorry we can't all have the perfect life."

"Are you serious?" Knox balked. "You've never wanted this."

He scanned the Mavericks' General Manager's office. More spacious than most people's apartment, his best friend had a one-hundred-eighty-degree panoramic view of the stadium. "Not if retirement looks like a regular nine-to-five in a suit."

"Oh, is that what this is about?"

"Down, down." The baby handed the empty cup to Knox, as he leaned down to put her on the floor.

It was on the tip of Hawk's tongue to spill his guts. He was contemplating retirement. Health-wise, he didn't think he could play hockey much longer. Since Knox had already been through a lot with him, he didn't want to load more crap onto his friend's shoulders. "I'm not sure what's next."

"Dude, I've invested all your promo money. You don't need to figure it out anytime soon...if ever." Knox grabbed a half-bald doll from his desk and passed it to Sadie while her sister, Nyla, played with Hawk's shoulder-length hair. "What is this really about? Moe's? Because that dirty dive was overdue for a makeover."

Hawk turned his head away to hide his smirk, right into the face of the chubby-faced kid. She patted his cheek to console him, which was super cute but uber pathetic on his part. He sucked her little fingers into his mouth and opened his eyes wide. Nyla's uncontrollable giggles melted his heart.

"It's a lot of things, but that's definitely at the top of my list. And that freaking manager! Frosty, stuck-up—"

"Ooooh." The toddler put her other hand over his mouth.

"Mumm-mm-m." He playfully nibbled on her baby hand.

"Huh, you and Moe's daughter must have hit it off."

"Daughter?" Hawk whipped his head in Knox's direction. "Moe doesn't have any kids." Similar to a body check on ice, the air was sucked straight out of his lungs.

"He does — and she's some sort of anomaly."

"Such as?"

Knox took a seat at his desk. "We haven't been back to Moe's since your Keating Cup run, which means I haven't had time to get all the details yet, but—"

"If she's so amazing, then why would she be working at the bar?" Hawk pouted.

"Hell, why do you?"

"Hell, hell, hell," Nyla chanted sweetly in his arms.

"Thanks for that," Knox grumbled. "Look... Obviously something is on your mind. How about we head over to Murphy's pub and work on your retirement plan?"

"Sure, but what about?" Hawk hung the toddler by her leg upside down and wiggled the little munchkin in the air. "Or did I miss when Murphy's turned kid-friendly?"

"Hell, hell, hell." Nyla giggled and wiggled in front of him.

"There's no way I can get any work done now. Grab the stroller and we'll sneak them in through the back door."

"If Remy asks," Hawk muttered, "I didn't know anything about this." He flipped the baby behind his back with one hand to a peal of sweet baby giggles that boomed in his ear. Not at all on board with this plan, he followed Knox's instructions to get the stroller.

Chapter Three

A harsh beam of sunlight streamed through her apartment window. In desperate need of caffeine, Lexi stumbled around her small kitchen, while Bloomberg Television played in the background.

She hadn't made it to the bar on time for at least a week. Sadly, she lived directly above Moe's and still managed to run late every single day. Weak from lack of sleep, or simply run down from life in general, Lexi didn't bother to explore which one weighed more heavily on her at the moment.

Tucking her flirty blouse into her pencil skirt, she tried to ignore the music that vibrated the floorboards underneath her bare feet.

The biggest mistake of her life had been marrying Josh. Of course, living above a blues bar seemed less serious in comparison but came dangerously close to nudging that fuck boy out of his numero uno position. In a few minutes Simone would hit the ceiling with a broom, a not-so-subtle hint for her to get her ass in gear.

As Lexi transferred her phone to her left hand, she grabbed her mug off the drip tray and took note of SugarTech stock's steady incline on the television. Before her public ousting, none of the company's developers had anything ready to test, let alone release. One slip-up, only one from either her idiot ex-husband or SugarTech's useless board of trustees, then she might have half a chance at getting her life back.

Three solid thumps to Moe's ceiling vibrated against the bottom of her feet. Lexi's time was officially up. After flinging the foam run-off from the top of her cappuccino with her fingertips, she slipped into her heels.

Lexi juggled her mug and gripped the doorknob as she glanced over her shoulder to see if she'd forgotten anything. The one-bedroom apartment had seen better days. A slutty film of eighties grime coated every nook and cranny. Since she hadn't planned on staying for any length of time, she left the funky décor in place. Maybe if its cheesy appearance annoyed her enough, Lexi would finally get her shit together.

She opened the door, then hurried down the stairs to the kitchen. Delightfully sweet laughter from the bar's longtime cook filled the galley.

"You'll get used to this yet," Peaches bubbled. Lexi hugged the dark chocolate woman from behind and kissed her cheek. Round in all the right places, she held onto to her a little longer than she should have.

"God, I hope not," she cooed in her ear. The best cook in the world patted her arm. Every morning she needed her daily dose of Peaches or she would lose her mind. After one more tight squeeze, Lexi walked to the swinging door to the bar and flung it open. "I'm here, I'm here—"

"And late, I might add." Hawk gestured between himself and Simone, while the jarring sound of a needle sliding off the record bellowed inside her head. "That's just unprofessional. I mean, how do you think that looks to the rest of us?" Raising his thick eyebrow, the big dude from the previous night seemed to actually wait for an answer.

Smug muthafucka, was her first thought. *Don't stare at his square jaw and perfectly symmetrical face,* quickly turned into her second.

"Looks like you did in fact talk to my manager," she told him. Moe had called her last night, insisting she keep the big crybaby. The deal those two had between them made no sense, but she didn't want to press the point.

"Sure did." He leaned his muscled arm against the bar and tossed her a big, toothy grin. The short sleeves of his T-shirt left nothing to her imagination. This man was a perfectly cut specimen of peaks and valleys. "It's funny how you didn't mention he was your daddy."

Lexi's phone vibrated in her hand. "Considering there was a large maniac screaming at me in a bar full of people, it must have slipped my mind," she muttered before she dropped her eyes to her screen. A countdown that began at twelfth hour took over her home menu. No doubt it was a ploy by her ex to goad her.

Evidently putting thousands of miles between them must have thrown a kink in his plans to needle her into a face-to-face confrontation. Lexi ignored her phone and placed her attention back on the real-life giant who continued to stare her down.

"Since you called Moe to tattle, please don't let me interrupt whatever it is" — she waved her hand wildly in the air — "you do around here." Lexi spun on her heels and headed to her office. The man seemed pumped to go a few more rounds with her, but if she factored her current mood into the equation, she knew he would probably win.

* * * *

As the seventeen-year-old tuned his guitar on stage, Lexi dropped a basket of Peaches' famous buffalo wings off at the booth in the corner. She had made a deal with a retired music teacher on the southside, who tutored in his spare time. If he taught his students blues, then they could play for Moe's lunch crowd.

A dozen hangers-on from the noon crush still lingered longer than usual. Peaches' appetizers were legendary and apparently were the sole reason Moe's doors had managed to stay open this long.

Stopping off at the bar, she picked up a mug of black coffee, while the young musician worked his way into Muddy Waters' *She Moves Me*. A gravely growl erupted from the kid's lanky body.

"What do you think?" She placed the cup in front of one of her father's old bandmates, Carl, aka Crazy Legs.

"Better than that last one," he grunted.

"There's nothing stopping you from giving them tips."

"Babysitting is not my thing." He picked up his mug and blew on the piping hot drink. "When's Moe coming in?"

Lexi didn't have an answer for him. Instead, she took in the kid's clean tone and strong command of the room. "This one's got something." She patted the old man on the back. "Talk with him. I think he'll appreciate it."

"Humph, maybe," Carl grunted.

Behind on paperwork, she headed to her office. Lexi still needed more servers, preferably ones who wouldn't rob them blind. The alert from her phone vibrated against the top of her desk. She glanced down at the screen — four hours had passed on the countdown.

An uncomfortable bubble of dread churned in her stomach. There was nothing a narcissist hated more than the perceived loss of control. Quick to extinguish the flame of anxiety Josh wanted to create, she opened her desk drawer and placed her cell inside, slamming it shut.

"Who's on a first-name basis with their parents?"

Lexi's head jerked up to find problem number two in her crosshairs. Hawk leaned against the doorway, shooting her a lazy smirk she'd fought hard to ignore the entire day.

"That sounds like a question for Moe." She trained her face into a blank slate, devoid of emotion. Lexi wished she could say the tech world had taught her that trick, but unfortunately that particular talent was a holdover from her shitty marriage.

"It's just curious I've worked here for a few years and haven't seen you, not once?"

As Hawk graced her with a lopsided smile, bright specks of brown and green twinkled in his hazel eyes. Similar to a bad kid, mischief was written all over his pretty mug. Maybe in another life she would have played with him, but unfortunately Josh had stomped out any sort of good humor.

"That is another question for Moe. So far you're batting a thousand."

"Well, let me hit you with one that you can answer." He pushed off the door and brought a picture frame from behind him. "Why did you hide all this awesomeness in the stockroom?" Standing smack in the middle of sexiest people she'd ever laid eyes on, the big guy held up a trophy.

"Ah, what sport is that?" she asked, completely in the dark.

"Hockey."

Imagining the man spinning a graceful figure eight, she coughed into her hand, hiding her chuckle. "Correct me if I'm wrong, but Moe's is a blues bar, right?"

"Got it. I'm no Louis Armstrong, but I'm a championship winner — and Chicago loves their winners."

Arrogant much? She bit her lower lip to stop all the smart remarks from flying out of her mouth. "Blues and hockey aren't exactly peanut butter and jelly."

"Point," he sighed, evidently done with dispensing the charm.

"They don't mix." Lexi leaned back in her seat. "Honestly, these people probably think you're just a really big bartender."

"Then you should hang this up." He held the picture of all the beautiful people higher. "In the main bar — to prove them wrong."

Her phone buzzed inside her desk again. No matter how much the puck molester provided a good distraction, Josh would never let Lexi forget that he existed.

"How's this..." She tapped her finger against her head in quiet contemplation. "And I'm just spitballing here, but why don't you learn to sing the blues?"

Faster than the beats of a bumblebee's wing, his affable mask of sweetness dissolved. "Okay, lady... What the hell is your problem?" he asked, stepping closer to her desk.

Rhetorical? That was rhetorical, right? Since all six-foot-four inches of the answer loomed above her.

"It's obvious not many people tell you no, so why don't you go cry to Moe? Then, pick a spot to stick that picture, preferably up your—"

"Ma, Pa"—Simone peeked her head in her office doorway with a tense smile—"we hate it when you fight." She lowered her voice. "Seriously, you two psychos, we have customers."

"I'm out of here." Hawk tossed the framed picture onto the leather couch and took off.

Stepping farther into the room, Simone shut the door behind her. "What did I tell you?"

Ah crap. Lexi hated Simone's 'go to the corner' reprimands. Hoping to make it easier on herself, she averted her eyes to focus anywhere but the normally sweet bartender's face.

"Hey." Simone snapped her fingers close to her nose. "That trick doesn't work for my five-year-old. What makes you think it's going to work for you?"

"Mehmehmehmeh," she rushed out in a stream under her breath. "Cause I'm grown."

"Not from where I'm standing."

What the hell? Did this woman have super elf hearing?

"Look." The Mohawk-sporting, five-foot-nothing woman placed her palms flat on her desk and smooshed her cute little face in front of hers. "That shiny remodel you did out there was well needed, but this place doesn't work without Sugarfoot Mosely's blues, Peaches' amazing appetizers and that sexy ass man who just walked out of here."

"He's not that sexy," Lexi muttered.

"Gurl, did that divorce screw with your eyesight?" She cocked her head to the side, causing her asymmetrical hair to flop into her thick lashes. "Because you ain't looking hard enough."

Chapter Four

Once again, Hawk found himself walking to clear his head. Chicago's August was unpredictable. Mild weather was every city-dweller's dream, but a humid attack of brutality was generally what the masses received, whether they wanted it or not.

Summer was winding down, and he had three more weeks until training camp. Hawk had no idea why he allowed that woman any room to get under his skin. It might have had something to do with the way he grew up, but he wanted to lay blame at Lexi Waters' feet and nowhere else.

For him to have bagged a cheerleader was a no-brainer. Even though he was an orphaned kid, he'd still had his pick of the geeks, goths and popular girls.

No one had wanted to turn down the only biracial orphan who not only played sports but conquered them. He had that 'bad boy misunderstood' thing down to a science. However, there was one group who wouldn't give him the time of day. No matter how hard he'd tried, the beautiful, brainy girls paid him dust. Not to be confused with the nerd or the chick next door — those two groups were either awarded smartest or most popular in the yearbook.

The beautiful brain was a self-defining chick who always scored most successful. For the life of him, he couldn't figure it out, but he'd finally settled on that thing called a path. Most successful girls never deviated from the path nor would they tool around with a guy who didn't have one. After a while, he had a sixth sense for those type of chicks and steered clear of them.

Hawk may not have known one single solitary thing about Moe's secret daughter, but what he did know was that the 'most successful' title oozed from her pores.

"Thought I would find you here." He crossed through the lush grass and headed straight for Sugarfoot Mosely. The bright rays from the sun illuminated his dark brown skin. Moe dug his hand into the bag on his lap. He tossed bread into the pond, causing a raft of ducks to float closer.

"Breaktime already?" Moe asked, tossing out more crumbs.

"What the hell? I've been gone for almost two months, and when I come back, you have a full-grown kid?" *One who resembles a video girl from the late nineties or early two thousands*. He had pinpointed that exact era due to the immeasurable amount of time he'd spent spanking his meat to those videos.

"Call me foolish, but I was hoping you two would get along for more than five minutes."

The ducks paddled in the water in front of them. Hawk popped a squat next to the blues legend and took a deep breath. The day was unbearably hot in every way imaginable. "Talk, old man. You owe me that much."

"Lexington's mother was a dancer with the circuit," Moe began. "We would bump into each other from time to time."

"Literally, I take it?"

Moe chuckled. "Something like that. We weren't anything serious — or at least not on my end."

"Where you laid your hat was your home?" Hawk quoted The Temptations' *Papa Was a Rollin' Stone*.

"How did you know that song was made for me?" They laughed. Moe's cat-daddy existence chipped away at the irritation that had jump-started his mood moments ago. The blues singer always had that effect on him, and that's why it had hurt when he'd found out about Lexi. Evidently, they weren't as close as he'd believed.

"After the gold-digging monster popped up pregnant, I wasn't at the top of my game anymore, but I was still riding a good wave. Outside of music, not too many things got my attention. Anyway, she ended up using the kid for an ATM, but after a while, I finally got tired of her yoyo antics. Lexi's the reason I settled down and bought the bar — to gain full custody, I needed the appearance of a stable household."

"Hmmm, and here I thought you were a playboy for life." A prodigy at a young age, Moe had played with the best of them. His career spanned the late sixties to the eighties, with the occasional resurgence. Hawk had assumed the lull in his career was due to his music category and not a secret daughter.

"For a long, long time I was... But then I started to hear things."

"What are we talking about here? Abuse?" Hawk reached over and grabbed a handful of stale bread.

"More neglectful than anything. I tried to get custody after I found out the kid was pretty much taking care of herself, but her mom didn't want those checks to stop."

"A story for the ages." Hawk threw his crumbs toward the squirrels. Since the fuzzy rats were far more entertaining than the feathered swimmers, he permitted them a handout.

"Yeah, I didn't invent that shit." Moe grabbed his cane that he'd rested against the bench and stood up. "She sent Lexi off to some genius school the kid didn't even want to go to—and the rest is history." He hobbled closer to the pond's edge and dumped the rest of the bread into the water. "Look… I don't want to talk ill of the dead, but Satan got himself a new bride when that woman kicked the bucket."

As Hawk laughed at his macabre joke, Moe pulled a handkerchief out of his pocket and dabbed at his forehead. The humidity was probably doing a number on the old man's blood pressure. The oppressive air was thick enough for a good backstroke.

"Lexi is independent, unbelievably smart and most of all private. My career always felt like it was embarrassing to her. Anyway, I gave the kid some space. I guess I didn't want to harsh her mellow?"

"Nobody says that. Who says that?" Hawk rolled his eyes at Moe's hippie-dippy slang.

"There's more, but I'm tired and hot—"

Hawk stood to leave. "No prob, we'll rain check the rest of that story and I'll walk you home." It was still early. After he dropped Moe off, he would check out what his boys were up to for the night. Too many things had changed in a short amount of time, and he found himself miles away from clean ice to glide on.

"Be nice to her. Lexington is a lot like glass—easy to break but can still kill you."

"What are you talking about? I'm nice to everyone." Hawk snorted. He wasn't the one who had a whole freaking kid and hadn't told anybody.

"Uh-huh." Moe took off at a super-speedy negative five miles per hour clip across the park. "However nice you think you are, ratchet it up by ten, then we'll at least have a jumping off point."

"Fine, but if you don't limp faster, old man, it'll take me until next week to work on being that insincere mofo you want me to be."

* * * *

The day had gone by in one big blur. A server on the afternoon shift had called off, and one of Simone's kids had come down with symptoms that had eerily resembled the bubonic plague. After she'd downed several cups of coffee, Lexi had managed to pump enough gas in her tank to close the bar.

"Goodnight, boss."

She waved at one of the last kitchen servers to leave before she knelt down and scrounged around for wood polish.

As she grabbed the towel and clean can from underneath the counter, her phone went crazy above her head. Bells chimed, which shouldn't have been possible since she had put it on silent hours ago.

A knot of dread yanked inside her gut.

Lexi straightened and stared at the face of her cell and *00:00:00* ran across her screen. Josh had already taken pretty much everything — her money, intellectual property — and if he had his way, her entire business. *What's left?* Snatching the phone off the back counter, she pressed her thumb onto the home button.

Assaulted by naked images of herself, a suffocating burn of acid inched its way into her throat.

While her breasts swung to a melodic beat in the video, Lexi's eyelids fluttered closed. It was a perfect HD shot of her naked body. Without a shadow of a doubt Lexi knew she would be the one and only star in this porno. Text froze in front of her underwhelmed expression.

Want to see the rest?

A sonic boom seemed to radiate inside her head. On the surface, the video barely computed. Intense pain surged through her system, causing a sensory overload. Lexi gripped the phone. Conflicted by the wealth of emotions that raged inside of her, she sank to the floor.

Swiping at the hot tears that streamed down her cheeks, she choked back a sob. She hated crying, but even she had her limits. Josh wanted her share of the firm. The video violated the morality clause in the company's contract. Of course, he would never admit that the other star in the film was him.

After five minutes, she would get up. *No wallowing allowed.* Unfortunately, her legs didn't get the memo, and her whole body went jellyfish. No longer able to outrun the weight of the world, she was paralyzed by her circumstances and stayed planted on the bar-room floor.

"Hey, it's Hawk. I'm just going to take a load off next to you for a minute," he said softly.

Lexi didn't know where he'd come from or how long he'd been there, since she couldn't see past the wealth of tears that streamed down her face. Of course, it wouldn't have mattered. She could pick the big guy's scent out of a dark room full of people — sandalwood, musk and something sweet she couldn't identify. The man smelled deliciously different every time she encountered him, which she super wished wasn't at this devastating moment.

"I'm not vain enough to think the little disagreement we had earlier has sent someone as perfect as you into a soppy puddle on a barroom floor — "

Against her will, she chuckled at his assessment of the situation. She would have to be half out of her mind to sit on the place patrons pretty much considered their own personal toilet.

Sniffling, she tried to use the back of her hand to wipe her nose, but he stopped her.

"Hold on a sec. It looks like you should have been playing ball alongside Knox and Andre." He gently took her hand and covered it with a cloth napkin.

When did I start bleeding?

"Your father mentioned you're into tech stuff. I don't know how good you are, but I think this phone is done for." He placed her shattered cell onto her lap.

The instant reminder of her shitshow of a life had caused another wave of tears. Her heart slammed hard into her chest, shattering into a million pieces. Hawk gathered her close with his strong arms and held her.

A perfect stranger comforted her better than the man she had spent the last ten years of her life with. That realization made her sob even harder.

Chapter Five

After he'd won several rounds of pool at Murphy's Pub, Hawk called it a night. He usually spent his weekends at Moe's, but unforeseen forces of the type-A variety had put a damper on those plans. He stepped out of the flashy sports bar that had steadily filled up with patrons.

"Hey, Hawk." Penny Lane—he'd almost called her by the wrong name—sucked on her vape. The guys in the bar had coined her by the famous groupie moniker. It was dickish of them, to say the least, but she never knew when to call it a night. She blew out a stream of smoke. "Checking out early?"

He offered her a soft smile. "Yeah, it's getting kind of full in there."

"Need some company?" She pushed off the side of the bar to play with the collar of his jean shirt.

"No, I'm good. Do you need a cab?"

Her blue eyes didn't sparkle in mirth. Instead, they seemed dull.

"For a big, bad dude, you've always been the sweetest. No, I'll wait and see if the night takes a turn for the better."

"Sure." Hawk gave her a brotherly pat on the shoulder before he stepped away. "Take care of yourself." He never wanted to be the last guy hanging around way past closing time. Hawk seriously hoped that wasn't him in any aspect of his life—but mainly his career.

A little foggy in the head from the annoying techno music that Murphy's played all night made him appreciate the sweet music from Moe's. The blues bar vibe had always been easy for him to settle into. His regulars enjoyed reliving the good old days—or even the music nerds who swarmed the place on weekends. Total respect from both sides had been the glue that held their rag-tag little gang together. That's why he'd always hung out at Moe's, but since everything in his life was rolling toward change, this had become one more thing for him to reconsider.

Used to a daily routine, Hawk would take the heavy crap out of his pockets and leave it under the bar. That's how he'd found himself heading back to Moe's, hoping Simone hadn't left for the night. Sleeping on the park bench held zero appeal for him.

Hawk had tried to call the bar but got no answer. Thankfully, when he arrived, the door wasn't locked.

Before he walked in the dark room, a bone-chilling wail had forced a momentary stutter in his step. Frightened into motion, he headed straight for the source.

He had moved passed the chairs that were already stacked on the tables toward a soft whimper. Taking tentative steps, he peered over the mahogany wood of the bar. Huddled on the floor in a pitiful ball was the woman who had been on his mind all day — and not in a good way.

"Lexi?" he called her name. Afraid she was in shock, he stepped around the bar and knelt close. "Hey, Lex." She was too far gone in pain and her shoulders shook while the tears streamed down her angelic face.

For the briefest of moments, he managed to snap her out of her misery, but that ended the minute he stupidly placed her phone onto her lap. Unprepared for this fresh onslaught of tears, Hawk wrapped his arms around her dainty frame, pulling her close. Not well equipped to deal with this, he did the first thing that came to mind and talked.

"This is new territory for me. Usually I'm to blame if tears are falling or tires are being slashed, so allow me to freeball it here. I'll blabber about myself until you feel better and want to kick me out." Thinking that would receive some sort of response, he didn't expect more crying. "I'm not big on change, and in a short amount of time a lot has…changed. Those people in the picture are my family — and well, Moe was supposed to be in it but he was sick at the time — "

Word vomit tumbled out of his mouth. He didn't know where it came from, but he continued to blather in hopes she would stop crying. Hawk smashed grown men's heads for a living but holding this broken princess in his arms made him feel helpless.

"Next year will be up in the air for me. While everyone's life is progressing at a natural pace, mine is at a standstill. Then there's this place… A few years back, Moe's became my home away from home."

At some point the tears had dried up but she remained quietly tucked against his side. Here and there he heard her take little puffs of breath. From the way she'd squared off against him earlier, he didn't get the impression she was easily reduced to tears. Whatever had knocked her down must have been one hell of a doozy.

"The team I was on back then crapped out of the playoffs in the first rounds, and who knows where Knox was back then. It was a fluke that I stumbled into this place. Perfect food, great music and no one recognized me —"

"Hockey and blues don't mix." Lexi sniffed after repeating her words from earlier.

Surprised she was even listening, he smiled.

"Apparently, but I kept coming back anyway. Moe must have figured since I was around so much, he might as well put me to work. I've been playing bartender in the off seasons. It helps keeps my mind busy. Plus, I love this place."

She pulled away from him and sat up, and he instantly missed her warmth. "The renovations became one more thing to catch me off guard. I took it out on you, and I apologize for that." He tilted his head in her direction, which granted him a good whiff of her hair. Apricots, peaches and sunshine filled his nose. Hawk cleared his throat, not wanting to skeeve her out. She had already been through enough.

"So I propose we start over. My name is Hawthorne Maze, and I promise not to be a dick to you anymore." He put out his hand for her to take.

After a moment, she put her soft palm into his. "My name is Lexington Waters, and I promise not to let you be a dick to me anymore."

He shook her dainty hand with a chuckle.

Chapter Six

Moe's was packed to the gills. Word about the teen performers had spread. The afternoon rush had lingered well after the three-p.m. cool-down period. Lexi enjoyed the crush of people, but the servers needed a break.

Everyone's favorite little neo-soul singer took the stage to rapt applause as she grabbed the mic and belted out Billie Holiday's *Strange Fruit*. A tiny girl dressed in baggy clothes playing an upright bass held everyone's attention in the bar.

"No more TV, pretty lady?"

Lexi cleared the table and replaced Al's drink with a fresh one. Moe's regulars usually hung out in the game room until the crowd thinned out.

"Do you want to watch the news, Big Al?" Lexi searched for the remote. The servers never put the stupid thing back in the holder.

"Naw." He shook his head. "Curious is all. You were glued to it when you got here."

Not too long after she'd had her off-the-rails meltdown, Lexi had officially given up. The one thing Josh had wanted and didn't get was her shares in the company. Lexi owned fifty percent of SugarTech. The rest of the stock was split between Josh and the board. Even if the company's bylaws allowed for her dismissal, they couldn't do anything without her vote. Josh obviously wanted to change that and wasn't above blackmail to make it happen.

"That stuff can rot your brain." Lexi gathered trash off a freshly vacated table and placed it on her tray. "Let me know if you need anything else."

SugarTech's initial boom had allowed her to send Moe money once a month. Thankfully, he had lived off his music residuals and ended up saving the cash. After her divorce, Lexi didn't have a dime to her name. Her dad's stash had pretty much saved her, financially speaking. She'd covered the renovation cost with his rainy-day fund.

As Lexi walked into the main hall, the neo-soul singer strummed her bass. The whole bar was under this kid's musical spell. At least one good thing had come out of the implosion of her life. Lexi traded her tray to a passing server and stopped dead in her tracks at the sight of Hawk's championship picture that had come to life.

"Wow, the pretty people." The front cover of *Vanity Fair's* Hollywood Edition turned in her direction. Lexi didn't realize she'd spoken out loud.

"Says Moe's beautiful daughter. Hi, I'm Remy." The cinnamon-colored beauty waved. "I'm the wife of the big man's best friend."

Lexi stood dazzled by the group. They all seemed familiar, but she couldn't put her finger on why. In the past, she'd been too busy working to notice much more than coding. *Head-in-the-sand syndrome* is what Josh had called it. Obviously, it had worked in his favor.

"Hey, I'm Knox." A beautiful White guy with sparkling blue eyes pushed out of the swinging kitchen door, holding a tray of chicken wings in his hand. "Sorry about raiding your kitchen, but Peaches is a little backed up and Andre gets pushy without his protein." He took one of the baskets off the tray and slid it across the bar to a toffee-skinned, fine-ass man.

"Mmm-m, Peaches' wings are the best. Thank God you kept my girl back there." Andre shook the drumette toward the kitchen door. "Otherwise, I would have to ditch this place." He rolled up the sleeves of his long-sleeved, designer shirt. "Nice reno by the way. I bet there was a ton of nineties dirt and smoke they had to scrape off the walls before they got started."

"Watch your mouth!" Hawk barked. His bushy brows knitted together in one big, angry caterpillar line, while Andre smacked obnoxiously on his food.

"The whining Dirt McGirt must have done when he saw that you tore down his pig pen."

"Ignore my husband. He gets crazy hangry in the afternoon and Hawk is an easy target." An ebony version of Jessica Rabbit extended her multi-colored nails in her direction. "Lashonda."

As Lexi took the woman's Crayola-styled hand, she felt small in the presence of this gang of cool kids. Usually her mind was too busy trying to figure out products that would help monitor insulin, heart and blood pressure levels all at the same time. Even a makeup app that would put cosmetologists and the color-blind ignorant together had materialized in the limited-girl's mind. Her biggest hit had been the program that matched clothing stylists with everyday people and their lackluster closets. However, her unwarranted dismissal from her own company and board, allowed strange insecurities to seep into her psyche and whisper hateful words of failure in her ear.

"This pixie cut." Lashonda reached out and touched the tip of one of her short waves. "It's updated Betty Boop à la Toni Braxton…amazing. Remy?"

"Love it."

"Uh, I just…" Not used to such sweet, unsolicited compliments, she didn't know if she could trust them or not. "Cut it. First time I ever went this short…" Thrown by Remy's dazzling smile, Lexi petered off.

"Hey, what are you doing Saturday?" Behind the woman with the super-model good looks, Hawk bugged his pretty eyes open wide. Remy glanced over her shoulder at him before he ducked his head in the opposite direction.

"Say you're busy," Lashonda whispered on her way past. More graceful than she could ever be in heels that high, the video vixen of the group had already crossed to the opposite end of the bar.

"We're throwing this thing for charity." Remy turned back, pinning her with an intense stare. "You should come."

"Okay, s-s-sure."

"You won't regret it." Andre chuckled while he licked the buffalo sauce off his fingers.

A shiver of cold ran up her spine as an undercurrent of strange tension pulsed through the group, and she decided to ignore the 'odd man out' feeling that washed over her. "Is there something I should bring?"

"No," Remy cooed, running her hand through her long, silken strands with a far-off gaze. "Your favorite workout gear will suffice. We're playing dodgeball."

"Body cast," Knox coughed out.

"Medical insurance," Lashonda muttered.

"Sure hope your little ass can throw," Andre snorted in between his evil overlord-type cackle.

Confused and admittedly a little scared, Lexi locked eyes with Hawk over the bar. She could have sworn pity warmed his hazel gaze. *What the hell?* She quietly freaked out. *It's dodgeball!*

"Hey, if you're not athletic, it's no big deal. You'll be a backup," Remy told her.

As the small group laughed hard—a little too hard for her taste—that instinctual tingle of doubt rolled into a solid rock and felt heavy in her gut. Andre practically choked on his second basket of buffalo wings laughing hard at...what? *My demise?*

* * * *

Dog days of summer in Chicago were no joke. Most people sought out air-conditioned shelter. Remy's annual dodgeball charity event took place two weeks prior to the beginning of Eastern Loyola College's fall semester. A pretty neighborhood accommodated the college-age youth from the bustling city.

Saturday mornings on the college campus were fairly quiet this time of year. Hawk waited outside the gym, hoping to talk Lexi out of this massacre. Maybe they could go to breakfast or take a walk on the lake front—anything, and he meant anything, other than dodgeball.

"What are you doing!"

"Shit!" he cursed. Caught off guard, Hawk turned around to face one of the three stooges. Yes, he understood that made him a stooge—and no, he wouldn't admit that out loud.

"Why are you stalking the front door?" Andre chuckled with a mouthful of popcorn. For the smallest one in the group, Andre never stopped eating. The asshole dug deep into his Garrett's Popcorn bag, while he continued to eye him over the sack.

"Huh? What? No, I-I-I'm—"

"Remy will kill you—and I mean kill." The grimy *mutha fucka* plopped a handful of caramel and cheese kernels in his mouth from the Chicago mix, then gleefully chomped away.

Hawk shoved his head in front of Andre's smug face. "If you snitch, I swear to God I will—" Unlike anyone he'd ever known, Andre could burrow his way underneath his skin and irritate the shit out of him.

"Come on, you two! The damn game hasn't even started yet." Knox slapped him on the back and stepped past him to slide in next to Andre. "At least wait until the first round." He flipped the sunglasses down from the top of his head to hide the dark circles under his eyes.

"Don't take this the wrong way," Hawk said, "but you look like shit."

"Baby has colic and Remy is..."

"Training," Andre offered.

"Insane," Hawk countered.

"Probably pregnant," Knox grumbled. He brought his coffee to his lips and took a sip after he dropped that bomb.

"Yesss," Andre hissed. "This game has gotten soooo much better."

"Wow, man." Hawk didn't feel the slightest bit sorry for his friend. "Irish twins... You are definitely going to get your four in no time flat. So do you think maybe Remy should sit this game out?" He threw up a silent prayer, hoping Knox would agree with him.

"Noooo!" Andre screamed.

"And have her use my head for the actual ball? You must be crazy." Knox dug his knuckle into his eye before he took another swig from his Starbucks' cup.

"Romeo here was just about to tell his boss...crush...to run."

"Seriously, Hawk?" Knox moaned.

"No, not crushing," he rushed out. *And what if I am?* This evil dodgeball game would certainly put the kibosh on any reciprocal feelings on Lexi's part. "She's been through a hard time, and I just want to—"

"Make her feel better with your dick," Andre cut him off.

"Comfort her with your mouth," Knox offered.

Avoiding their wide-eyed, goofy stares, he checked over his shoulder to see if Lexi had made it to the campus parking lot and let out a hiss. "Shitheads."

"Fine... It's too damn hot to be out here." Swiping his arm across his brow, Knox wiped the dripping sweat off. "Suggest a fake injury, but don't warn her to leave. Remy will kill you." Knox tapped Andre on the shoulder and nodded toward the door.

Hawk waited for them to go into the gym before he dug his phone out of his pocket. Maybe she was still at the bar and he could catch her.

"How big is this thing? I thought it was a small event...you know, for kids?" He turned toward the sweet sound of her voice. Dressed in a pink tank top and yoga pants, the sight of the pretty bar owner made the corner of his lips twitch upward. Forcing his eyes to not drift away from her kewpie-doll-shaped face to check out her sweet body, Hawk had to concentrate.

As the sun caressed her warm, brown skin, little wet curls covered the top of her head. He didn't want to come off like one of those perverted leeches she dealt with on a daily basis at Moe's. However, despite the impending danger they were both about to put their lives in, Hawk couldn't contain his smile. *Fuck, she's hot!*

"Want some breakfast?" Grabbing her shoulder, he turned her in the opposite direction.

"What?"

"Yeah, this thing won't be starting on time." He led her away from the gym.

"But Remy said —"

Blood rushed through his veins in a flight or fright response. "We can get a quick bite, then come back —"

"Hawk!" Remy called out somewhere nearby.

"Shit!" His insides locked. Picking up his speed, he rushed them into the opposite direction.

"I swear, Hawk."

What the hell? He was a world-class athlete, who'd brought two Olympic medals and a championship trophy to Chicago. *How can my best friend's wife strike fear in my heart worse than a six-foot-six-inch hockey player?*

"Left something in the car," he lied.

"Is that so?" Remy stepped in front of them with her gang of batshit crazy preschool moms. "Could have sworn I passed by your motorcycle in the lot."

"Gwarkwahhh." He worked his mouth, but unintelligible words slipped out.

"Hey, girl, glad you came." The powder keg of crazy reached out to interlock her arm with Lexi's. "Why don't I take you inside while Hawk figures out what he needs from his ghost car?"

Remy and her gang yanked Lexi from his grip.

As he trailed behind, Hawk's boss-crush peered over her shoulder with a confused expression and wide eyes. Powerless to help her, he did the only thing he could.

"Run," he muttered to her. "Fucking *run*."

Chapter Seven

Trapped between *Black Panther's* Dora Milaje guards, Lexi snuck a glimpse over her shoulder. The concern from a moment ago had been replaced with stark horror—or maybe it was closer to pity that she read on Hawk's big, strong face.

"Don't listen to him. This is nothing more than a friendly game of dodgeball for charity."

"A squeamish hockey player... Where do they make them?" Everyone laughed at the pre-school mom's joke.

She tried ignoring the spindly fingers of nerves that crept along her spine while they stalked the empty halls of the college gymnasium before they stopped at the double doors.

"Honestly"—Remy held the metal handle in her grip—"you'll be nothing more than a bench warmer."

Isn't that what they tell kids before they get a vaccine shot? Don't worry. This won't hurt...and of course it's the worst pain they've ever felt in their entire little lives. Lexi wanted to ask why a six-foot-four-inch giant had freaked out about one puny game of dodgeball, when the sexy mom pushed the door open to a surge of screams.

"Oh wow, I thought this would be a..." Lexi faced an enormous crowd.

"We're playing for the animal shelter," one of the players said.

"Sorry, Charlie, but we're taking a vote this year."

As the women argued over which charity would get their winnings, Lexi took a seat on the nearest bench and instantly regretted not heeding Hawk's advice to put rubber to pavement and leave.

Wall-to-wall people covered the gymnasium. Lexi scanned the crowd. College students and what she figured were neighboring residents cheered from the bleachers. Face paint covered many of their psychotic faces.

"Uh, aren't they playing?" she asked one of the women closest to her. The crowd got louder when Hawk, Knox and Andre made their way to a cordoned-off area.

"Who?"

Lexi jerked her thumb in the direction of the hot alpha beasts' bleacher.

"Oh, that's the VIP section. Professional athletes aren't allowed to play."

"But—" The other side of the court filled up with men and women wearing Local 301 Fire Station T-shirts. Villainous boos filled the gym. Officially confused, Lexi caught Hawk's eye and saw that the frown on his face had deepened.

"Hey, gurl. Sorry, but I can't play." Lexi turned toward the sexy Amazon who had joined them at the bar the previous night. Lashonda—she recalled her name—rocked a crazy Nicki Minaj candy-colored wig and an arm sling.

"Are you serious?" Remy hissed.

"Yeah, I was styling a video shoot and must have wrenched it."

"Really, Shonda?" her husband hollered from the bleachers.

"Shut up, Dre!"

He waved her off as Remy slid her a nasty glare.

Without saying another word, Remy crossed the room toward the judges' table. Lexi assumed the burly dude who had sidled up beside her was the captain of the opposite team, but at this point she was pretty much in the dark about this whole event.

"This isn't at all what I thought it would be."

"Huh." Lashonda popped a squat on the other side of Lexi. "I can't believe you actually showed up for this shit."

"What?"

"Yeah, I could have sworn Hawk was going to warn you." She muttered something about misunder-standing a vibe before she shrugged. "Sorry."

"Why?"

"Oh, you'll see."

While Remy engaged in a heated discussion with the refs, Lexi made note of all the exits. *Would it be in bad form to ditch a charity event at the beginning? Or should I hustle my ass out closer toward the middle?*

The piercing sound from the ref's whistle pulled her attention to the gym floor. He signaled for the teams to join them. After the soccer moms finished their unbelievably limber stretches, they walked onto the court, meeting the opposing team at the dividing line.

"Welcome to the third annual northside dodgeball competition! We have the Ladybugs defending their home turf." The place went wild at the adorable name of the woman's team. "And the Local 301 Fire Station — " Boos rocked the stadium before the ref could finish his announcement.

The captain snatched the microphone. "Rules are the underlying fabric of our society. You can't go doing what you want willy-nilly without repercussions."

As the jeers grew louder, the ref took the microphone back.

"Players, please take your places."

Lexi hadn't witnessed this much drama at a professional basketball game. "This is the playoffs, and the fire chief tried to get the Ladybugs disqualified last year," Lashonda explained. "Then he tried to ban our team from playing in the tournament. Remy's little feud with Local 301 goes way back, and that's why I thought Hawk would have at least warned you."

The ref gave a quick rundown of the rules. "We have a substitution for the Ladybugs."

Completely clueless, Lexi scanned the gym for the extra player. When she felt the heated weight of a room full of eyes on her, she pointed her index finger at her chest.

"Yeah, hot nerd, you're up." Remy waved her onto the floor.

What the hell?

As she stepped onto the court, her attention was drawn back to the VIP section. Maybe she should reconsider that truce with Hawk. '*Sorry,*' he mouthed to her.

"Have no mercy," Remy told her once she joined the team. "And don't let those kids fool you." Lexi popped her head out of the huddle to see three girls who looked no older than thirteen lean into a runner's stance. "They seem sweet, but they're super-fast. The firefighters have strength but no speed."

The wall clock went down to zero before the ref blew his whistle. A blur of crazy activity took place directly in front of her. Regardless of her apparent egghead status, Lexi refused to be the first one knocked out.

According to the rules, she could use any ball that was still in play. She delicately tiptoed behind one of the Ladybugs who had already made a run for the ball, and Lexi caught it once it bounced off the blonde's chest.

As she hid behind another mom to dodge a million small weapons aimed at her body, she slung the ball she had in her hand. An avid video game player, Lexi immediately studied her opponent's strategy and went in for the kill.

A short twenty minutes of playing hard and fast felt closer to an hour. After Remy pegged one of those psychotically fast teenagers, she leaned into some sort of Matrix-type back bend. Thankfully, Lexi had artfully sidestepped a bullet that her opponent whipped in her direction and beamed the ball she held at the last firefighter standing.

A roar took over the gym. For the first time in her life, she'd won something that held no weight in the techie world. Most importantly, her achievement didn't hold the burning gaze from men who could make or break her career. It was a frivolous endeavor that she didn't know she'd be thrilled to win.

Overwhelmed by the loud cheering, Lexi hid her laughter behind her hand. Accepting her kudos from the rest of the team who rushed onto the court, she giggled her way to victory.

Chapter Eight

The dodgeball game winners and losers came together at Moe's in a surprisingly harmonious gesture to celebrate the Ladybugs' victory.

Since the pub was packed to the seams, her servers had to squeeze within cracks of space left between bodies. If nothing else ever went right in her life, at least Moe's had experienced a surge in customers. The sales line had finally eased well into the black.

"Hey." Remy slid next her.

"Are you going to help me serve drinks?" Lexi asked, pointedly arching her eyebrow. She had given the kids at the community center in California that same look a time or two. *Oh, how I miss those girls.* "Otherwise, Ms. Boss Lady..." Lexi nodded to the opposite side of the bar.

"Boss Lady... I like that." Remy nodded.

"Cool. I'll take Hot Nerd and you keep Boss Lady."

As she mixed a whiskey sour in the shaker, Remy grabbed a beer mug and turned toward the tap. "About that… I'm sorry, but the captain's misogynistic crap gets me every time."

The opposing team was supposed to pay the bar tab, but Lexi didn't hold out any hope that would happen.

"No worries. I've been called worse," Lexi said.

"I bet. There are not many women in the tech industry with your type of clout."

"Oh," she uttered in disbelief, "you know who I used to be?"

"Clothes were different than the last time I saw a pic of you." Remy glanced over her shoulder at her. "And that hair is definitely new, but nope, I would still place you in the bad-ass category." Remy threw her a quick wink. "Besides, it's my job to know things. But I have to admit that you've managed to keep one hell of a low profile."

"Yeah." Lexi poured the whiskey sour into a glass. "That was by design."

"Well, if I were you, I wouldn't want anyone to know that I could play with the big boys and beat them at their own game either."

Taken aback by her word choice, Lexi stopped mid-toothpick-cherry-stab and wondered if Remy knew more about her circumstances. A split among business partners had been announced at the beginning of the divorce, but she'd rarely dealt with the press, unlike her ex-husband.

While it was on the tip of her tongue to ask the stunner what she did for a living, Remy slid a beer over the counter.

"This isn't what I ordered," one of the firefighters from the game grumbled.

"But this one is so much better." Remy pouted. As her big eyes went soft, she stuck out her bottom lip.

"I, uh... I, uh," he stuttered, "think I want to keep this one, thank you."

"Your soo-o welcome." She smirked. The beer she handed to their opponent cost several dollars more than the one he'd originally wanted. Officially in awe of goddess Remy's manipulative tactics, Lexi forgot about the drink she had made.

"Ahem." The customer cleared his throat.

"Oh, sorry." She dropped the cherry in his whiskey sour and plunked it down in front of the man.

"What do you do for a living?" When Lexi glanced up, she found the sexy chameleon had already left the bar.

"We've been over this." Hawk scooched his big body into the spot where Remy had vacated. "I play on ice with a stick. Of course, I'm nowhere as skilled as your athletic prowess."

"That, I'm afraid, was a one-off," Lexi told him.

"Not from where I was standing." He reached around her to swipe an orange slice from the garnish tray, momentarily caging her body between his ripped biceps and the bar. Lexi held her breath to shield herself against the crisp, woodsy scent that wafted from his golden café-au-lait skin.

"To offset my man repellent nerdiness, my mom made me take ballet for years." She exhaled once he leaned away. "Sadly, video games helped me with the hand-eye coordination part."

Taking a page from Remy's book, Lexi poured an expensive foreign tap in a mug. She mistrusted her ability at flirting, but figured Hawk's towering presence might convince the customer to accept the drink without complaints. Besides, the douchebags who surrounded the bar had no problem chucking balls at her face less than an hour ago. *Fair is fair.*

"Hey, my woman needs a time-out. Can you watch the kidlets?" Knox squeezed in between the Local 301 losers, as she'd heard Remy call them.

"No can do, man. I've got camp."

"Shit," Knox hissed.

"*Whootosh.*" One of the firemen mimicked a whip, only to receive a smattering of giggles from his co-workers.

Knox faced the offender, who tried to duck behind his schooner of beer. "She literally just kicked your nuts in, and you assholes are making pussy-whipped jokes?" He held his fingers inches apart. "I was this close to almost feeling sorry for you." Knox snorted. "Hit me with the tap, Hawk."

"A time-out?" Lexi mumbled. "That's not sexist."

Hawk reached across her for what felt like the millionth time, to grab a clean mug. "Wait for it." He let off a throaty chuckle near her ear. "Just wait for it."

"Can you hear me?" Tapping the microphone, Remy stood on the stage where the old timers had stepped off moments ago. "As the leading winner of our annual dodgeball game…"

"Ladybugs!" someone screamed.

"For the third year in a row" — girly applause and feminine whistles were offset by manly groans in the bar — "this win would not be possible without Hot Nerd over there by the bar."'

"Remy!" Knox shouted.

"What?" She glared at him. "Lexi said she was totally cool with it. Right, gurl?"

"Uh?" Warmth spread up her neck and bloomed across her cheeks. If she were lighter, her embarrassment would have been more apparent. "It's fine." She waved off all the attention. "I'm good."

"Damn right she is." Remy pointed at her. "The other person this wouldn't be possible without is my husband, Knox."

"Here it comes," he grumbled before he knocked back half the mug of beer Hawk had set down in front of him.

"He gave a sizeable donation to the Local 301 to make sure Captain Gilroy would not file another baseless complaint against the Ladybugs," Remy told the crowd.

"Okay, n-now dammit, Remy, that is n-not what h-happened," the fire chief stammered from the opposite end of the room. "You are making that up. Furthermore, I'm not entirely sure that little gal you brought in wasn't a ringer of some sort."

Remy shot Lexi a wide-eyed glance to most likely confirm that the fire chief was indeed a misogynistic idiot.

"No hard feelings, Gilroy. All is well. I'll accept your apology for trying to get the Ladybugs banned from the competition."

"Ha," he bellowed. "I would never give you an apology."

"Is that so? Well, I invited a very special guest speaker who told me different. Ms. Gilroy?" The kitchen door opened to two Ladybug players escorting an elderly lady into the room.

"Mama!" he shouted, unable to shove his way any closer. "This is low, Remy, even for you."

"No, sir, I can go lower. In fact..." She signaled to someone in the back of the bar. The *Cha Cha Slide* beat dropped over the sound system. "How low can you go?" She held the microphone off the stage to the audience to sing along with the lyrics.

"Can you go down low?" they shouted back.

While the fire chief pushed his way through the packed room, Remy shimmied to the floor to the lyrics of the song. Once all the way down, she knelt on the edge of the stage and held the mic out for his mother.

"Tommy Gilroy, I didn't raise you to be such a sore loser."

"Oooohhhh," the bar instigated the older woman scolding her son.

Unable to force herself to stop this pitiful display of public shaming, Lexi laughed. A hard belly jiggle that she hadn't experienced for some time amused her to the point of tears.

"Now do you see?" Hawk chuckled.

"Nope," she hiccupped, wiping her eyes, "I'm still not convinced she needs a time-out."

* * * *

Styled in a fancy suit and tie, Hawk walked the backstage area of the United Center. Training camp had finally ended earlier that week. Tomorrow pre-season would officially begin, but today the front office wanted to parade the starting lineup on stage for the press and fans.

"Oscar Nyman!" the emcee called out the center's name to thunderous applause.

Hawk stepped past the craft food table, which was covered in junk—most of the rookies lived off of the empty calories. On the other hand, the veterans only ate fruits and vegetables. He plucked a couple of strawberries off the platter, then plopped one in his mouth. This small test of wills was a type of welcome to the pro's hazing. If the kidlets continued to eat crap, they would burn out fast.

Since his health was already compromised, he couldn't take any chances. Not to mention his damn-near-ancient age didn't do him any favors. Hawk had to play smarter, not faster than everyone else.

"Axel Larsson," the emcee announced.

Hawk stopped behind the thick backstage curtain and munched on a raspberry he had swiped as well.

On his way past, the kid flashed him a huge grin. "Let me show you how it's done, old man." The young idiot jogged onto the stage with an off-the-rack suit and a smarmy smile, sure to fool even the sweetest of the Northern Royals hockey fans. Shooting finger pistols at the crowd, the little shit did a fancy spin for the cameras.

"Now that one's going to be a problem. I can already see it on the wall." Coach Camden stepped beside him. They kept their eyes on Axel, who high-fived the fans nearest to the stage. "Maybe front office could tempt you into a coaching position?"

Hawk chuckled. He had no idea what he wanted to do once he retired, but babysitting the arrogantly stupid wasn't it.

"These rookies" — the gray-haired giant sighed. Weary was the best way Hawk could take in the defeated posture of his former hockey idol — "are very different from past generations, but I believe they may be able to relate to someone like you a little better than someone who's been out of the league since the ice age."

Hawk's text alert went off. He dug his phone out of his breast pocket and smiled at Lexi's text.

Not what you're used to, but let's see how you do with Ari Lennox, Solange Knowles and Summer Walker.

Unwilling to leave things lingering in the air between, Hawk had asked the bar manager about her musical influences — an ice-breaker of sorts to keep the door open for them to keep in contact without coming off like a cornball. Not much of a music connoisseur, he didn't listen to much other than eighties hair bands or grunge rock from the nineties. However, the influence of Prince, Lenny Kravitz and Jimmy Hendrix always had a spot on his playlist. He typed back —

Fine, but a report will be due on Sound Garden, Nine Inch Nails and Pearl Jam ASAP.

The orphanage hadn't had much in the way of entertainment. It wasn't until he'd won that golden Willy Wonka ticket to prep school that he was introduced to different music.

Naturally, he had gravitated toward the big-tittied blondes of the metal world and the sad-sack life of the grunge. As of late, he had become used to the old timey stuff the regulars played at Moe's, but when it came to the bastard love child of blues, he was an absolute novice. Over the past few months, Lexi had slowly integrated neo soul into Moe's steady rotation. He was intrigued not only by the music, he was captivated by the manager as well.

She responded —

LOL. If this is a challenge, trust me, I'll win.

Scoring anything less than a C results in an automatic retest.

Once he typed out his message, he put his phone back into his pocket.

"And finally, one of the most celebrated players in the league and a fan favorite," the announcer yelled.

Hawk stole a peek at the audience. The grand-mothers who had cheered him on at every home game screamed from the front row, waving their signs in the air.

"A freaking fan favorite? Those old nuts would sell you their adult grandchildren. You're more popular than the goalie or captain. Tell me, son. How the hell did you do that?"

Hawk straightened the sleeves on his suit jacket and rolled the kink out of his neck. "Face it, Coach. I'm just a charming mutha fucka!"

The old ladies stood, flashing their gaudy shirts that had his face on them.

"Enforcerrrrrr Hawthornnnnne Maze!" Determined to enjoy every second of what could be his last season, he took a minute to let it all sink in.

"Do me a favor, Hawk." The coach grabbed his shoulder, stopping him from his big strut onto the stage. "Consider my offer. I really think you can have a great afterlife in hockey." He patted him on the back before he stepped into the blanket of bright lights and applause from his Northern Royals' people.

Chapter Nine

Fat, sloppy snowflakes fell from the sky and coated the streets. At least an inch of snow blanketed the ground. Sipping on her minty hot chocolate, Lexi stared out of Moe's front window.

Her cell vibrated in her hand, and she glanced down at her screen. With no intention of speaking with her lawyer, she hit decline on the 310 area code. She was pretty sure her attorney wanted her to take a deal — something stupid where all the charges against her would be dropped if she relinquished her seat on the board or, at the very least, sold off her SugarTech shares. Lexi felt it best to ignore her.

Taking full advantage of their separation period, Josh had called her one night to talk. Instead, Lexi had ended up at his place, engaging in a humiliating dose of sub-par sex. Her lapse in judgment had allowed Josh to creatively edit himself out of the final cut of his latest attempts at blackmail.

If the public ever got hold of her poor re-enactment of Kim Kardashian's porn tape, Lexi's opportunity to reinvent herself in the tech field would go up into flames.

Always the type of person to get ahead of a problem, Lexi decided to change tactics and sit this one out. 'Let the cards fall where they may' probably wasn't the best strategy, but she no longer had any strength left for a fight. Her iPhone vibrated again. However, this time when she checked her screen, she smiled.

10,000 Maniacs, The Cranberries and Bush are not grunge. Try again.

Lexi laughed at Hawk's text. It had been a month since she'd laid eyes on him. Their debate over music categories and level of taste—or, in his case, lack thereof—helped her to avoid dwelling on matters beyond her control.

"Who's that?" Simone asked from her station behind the bar. Lexi had nearly forgotten she was still there.

"Huh?" Beyond embarrassed, she smoothed out an imaginary wrinkle in her pencil skirt. "I don't know what..."

Simone nodded at her phone. "That wouldn't be a famous hockey player by day, mediocre bartender by night...yay tall?" She lifted her hand well past her high, Mohawk-styled head of hair. "Super sexy."

"Why would you think—?"

"Please." She waved her protest away and set down a cup of coffee in front of Crazy Leg Carl, the only customer Moe's had left. "You aren't his type and he's not yours, which means you two are perfect for each other."

"Make that make sense?" She bit her lower lip to hide her smirk. Simone was way too perceptive for her own damn good.

"Some say it's science, but honestly, whatever you think is working for you or him, for that matter, obviously doesn't." Simone leaned against the back bar.

"Opposites attract?" Lexi asked.

"If you think you two are opposites, then sure."

"Considering he's my employee and I'm his employer" — Lexi switched from one high-heeled shoe to the other — "this conversation is purely hypothetical."

"Hawk doesn't cash his checks, soooo" — Simone reached under the bar to grab her purse — "argument rejected. I need to get going before the snow hits. What do you say, Carl? You want a ride home?"

The man grunted. Simone walked to the kitchen door and pulled her coat off the rack.

"Did it escape everyone's notice that it's the beginning of November?" Lexi stepped toward the window. The flakes crashed to the earth, picking up speed fast. "Why does the city look like this?"

Simone threw her knitted scarf around her neck with a snort before she walked over to Carl. "Spring and fall are iffy in these parts, but winter and summer always come in like a beast." The bartender helped the old man off his bar stool, then assisted him to the kitchen door.

"Welcome to Chicago," Simone muttered.

Carl threw a stingy wave in the air as the duo left her in the bar alone.

"Night," she called out. Lexi flinched from the sound of the metal back door slamming shut.

Thankfully, most of the cleaning had already been done. All she had left were the bar stools and floors. She knocked back the rest of her hot chocolate.

Unsure if the storm was a little blip or a huge blizzard, she contemplated finishing everything the next day. However, Lexi took comfort in the menial tasks. Flipping the stools onto the tabletops one by one, she calculated how many of her unfinished development projects would be up for grabs if SugarTech's board won their lawsuit against her.

Before she was unceremoniously dumped, Lexi had deleted twelve apps, one program to rival Microsoft Word and another to compete with the best accounting software from SugarTech's main server. She refused to allow them to profit off her creations. Deep in thought, she nearly missed the rusty creak from the back door.

"Hello?" she yelled out, clutching the top of the chair. She had finally made it to the short tables in the middle of the room. If someone broke into the bar, her best escape route was the front door, which was too far to be a viable option. "Hello!" The first note of SZA's *Broken Clocks* blared from the kitchen as her chest clenched in fear.

Heavy footsteps forced her to scan the room for a weapon. *Run, grab a weapon, run, grab a weapon.* Lexi was trapped in a video game that looped in her mind. When the kitchen door swung open, a dark silhouette filled the doorway. Lexi lifted the stool inches from the ground.

"Is this song about what I think it is?" Hawk stepped into the dimly lit barroom. While Lexi set the stool back on the floor and released a huge sigh of relief, an unfamiliar wave of happiness surged through her body.

"Depends." She foolishly grinned at the big beast. "What do you think it's about?"

After shrugging out of his leather jacket, he tossed it on top of the bar. "At first I thought she was singing about an affair, but the more I listened to it..." Hawk crossed the room, his white T-shirt stretched against his bulging pecs.

As he shoved his wavy, shoulder-length hair away from his face, Lexi's body responded to him in several different ways. Afraid she was drooling, she stopped shy of using the back of her hand to wipe her mouth. She had witnessed enough customers openly lusting after the man. Unlike many of those shameless creatures, Lexi wanted to hold onto the little bit of dignity she had left.

"This song's about a three-way. How does anyone make it sound..."

"Inevitable?" she offered.

"Sweet." Hawk stopped in front of her. "You were right about H.E.R. and Solange Knowles. They're good."

"Glad you approve." While SZA crooned about the days of the week, an invisible, electric charge sparked between them. Maybe she'd let her loneliness fester to the point of delusion. Every time he worked, she witnessed the big, sexy man flirting his way through the bar. However, Lexi felt that their attraction was mutual.

Mere inches apart, the giant peered down at her. His bright hazel eyes dazzled from beneath his thick, dark lashes. "The team finally got a day off." The first few cords of Ella Mai's *Trip* played over the rumble of his deep voice.

"And you thought you'd what, pick up a shift?" She smiled, amused that he'd found an R&B song, this time without her assistance.

"No." He took a small step closer. "I wanted to ask you what you thought about Oasis."

The prickle of goosebumps across her arms ran a shiver of excitement along the base of her spine. Beating back a smile, she sucked her lower lip into her mouth. There's no way in hell he wanted to know her opinion on the group Oasis during an epic Chicago snowstorm. Tired of mulling over the smallest of problems, she decided to go with her freshly acquired devil-may-care attitude and play along.

"*Wonderwall* was a bop."

"Personally" — he put his finger under her chin, tipping her head toward his, and a pulse in her pussy jumped — "I always felt *Champagne Supernova* was highly underrated."

"Disagree," she whispered breathlessly. "We're going to need an unbiased opinion to break —" Before she could finish, he swooped in to claim her, gently putting pressure on her lips.

It was a soft and sensual kiss, not at all what she'd expected from this giant of a man. Maybe if she hadn't been sex-free for close to a year, Lexi could have handled his chivalry better. Instead, she placed her hand on the side of his five o'clock shadow and parted her lips. Slipping her tongue into his mouth, she moaned from the strong feel of Hawthorne Maze against her skin.

Brazen, perhaps, but she had carried the weight of the world on her shoulders. The sexy man in front of her was the perfect remedy to hitting the off switch on her racing thoughts. The weightless feeling that took over her body sparked life between her legs. Without truly knowing if she could bottle this feeling, Lexi shoved her fingers into his wavy hair and pushed deeper into the big man.

Chapter Ten

When he'd left Murphy's Pub that evening, Hawk had had every intention of going home. Hopping into his truck, he'd lost all sense of direction and driven straight to Moe's. His plans for the night hadn't included the little blues bar. With the short amount of time he had off, Hawk wanted to use it to catch up with friends, but an edginess had sunken into his soul.

Tomorrow a couple of his teammates would be auctioned off at some charity function for the franchise. Hawk, on the other hand, had a sponsored meet-and-greet, then the Northern Royals were back on the road. With Lexi heavy on his mind, he wanted to settle the restlessness that had pulled him into her sphere by twisting his gut into knots.

Weeks had passed since the last time he'd seen her. Positive the distance between them had magnified his feelings, he'd driven his truck into the alley behind the bar. It hadn't slipped his mind that Lexi was not only his boss but was also related to one of his closest friends. Worst of all, that pesky title 'most successful' flashed brighter than a neon sign above her gorgeous head.

He'd avoided the web search that would tell him she was way too smart for him, but that gold member status perfume had always wafted off her skin. Determined not to embarrass himself further, he threw the truck in reverse but stopped when he caught Simone and Crazy Leg Carl leaving the bar.

"Shit." Without moving a muscle, he held his breath. Waiting until they were well out of sight, he turned off the truck and opened the door.

As he stepped into the heavy snow, he grabbed his phone out of his jacket pocket and pulled up iTunes.

Hawk walked to the back door, which was slightly ajar, and pulled the heavy door open. The lock probably hadn't engaged when Simone had left. He set a mental reminder to check it later. No longer interested in fighting the magnetic pull that had brought him to the bar, Hawk maneuvered around the steel kitchen island.

Attempting to come up with a conversation piece that didn't make him sound stupid, he worked on a whole sentence besides a monosyllabic *Hawk like girl, pretty.*

While he toyed with his phone to rock SZA, those wicked nerves threw a mean MMA-style fight in his stomach. The jitters were a telltale sign that he was a goober, but he didn't realize how big until he pushed open the door and set eyes on Lexington Waters.

After a few words were exchanged, the only thing he could focus on were those glossy, pert lips on that beautiful doll's face.

Not that Lexi's tight skirt, form-fitting sweater and knee-high, black boots held his attention, but mainly it was her plump lips that stayed at the forefront of his mind. Before he could explain all the reasons *Champagne Supernova* was technically the better choice, he took the liberty to feel her lips against his. *A simple taste of her skin,* he told himself, *then I will apologize and completely understand if she never wants me to step foot inside this establishment again.*

Prepared to pull away and offer his resignation, he was stopped by the soft caress of her hand. Lexi had gently drawn her palm down the side of his stubble before parting his lips with her tongue.

With his dick springing into a hard brick at her moan, he had no choice but to explore where the rest of the evening would take him. Initially, all he'd wanted to do was see her and perhaps talk, not get his rocks off. He had his pick of groupies for that, but he actually desired something meaningful.

She was soft and sweet, and he sucked on her tongue. *I can beat back the need of want, but for how long?* Lexi pulled away from his lips, slipping down to his neck. "Want to — ?"

"What?" Lexi asked, in a sexy, rough tone. The hottie pulled back to stare at him with those big doe eyes as she grabbed his crotch. His dick hardened to an uncomfortable degree... He needed relief.

The guttural instinct to pound her pussy into oblivion overwhelmed his senses. Uptight and always put together, he didn't anticipate her assertive attitude. Hawk expected a King Kong-Fay Wray type of reaction — that whole damsel in distress response, not the *Basic Instinct* interrogation scene that he received.

"No. Uh…" He leaned his head against hers, hoping to slow down his freight train of emotions. "Talk?" The request sounded ridiculous to his own ears, considering he initiated this strange interaction in the first place. Hawk wanted to take things slow. He was too old to keep engaging in empty, one-and-done encounters.

"Okay." Lexi's warm breath tickled his neck. "What about? Oh, I know, we can discuss the impact Napster had on the music industry?" Quicker than an Olympic sprinter, she unzipped his jeans and slipped her hand into his pants.

"Ahh-h." He swallowed. Many things collided in his mind once her soft palm clutched his dick.

"Is that what you want to talk about? Or would you like to lay me down on this table and fuck me good?"

As tingles of warmth ran up his spine, Hawk gathered her close. "Napster destroyed the music industry as we knew it." He kissed his way up her neck while she pulled his cock out of his pants. The sensation of her dainty hand choking his stiff rod shot warm tingles throughout his core. "However…" He picked Lexi up and plopped her down on the table. Wanting to make his intentions perfectly clear, he leaned his face close to hers to stare into her pretty, brown eyes. "The Internet allowed independent artists to shine. And yes, I want to fuck you on this table."

"Look at that," she whispered. "We agree on something."

Unable to wait another freaking second longer, Hawk seized her beautiful lips with his. Everything about this woman turned him on. Desperate for another taste of her minty chocolate lips, he slipped his tongue into her mouth and leaned into her body.

Lexi's breasts pressed into his chest. Ready to explore every part of her, Hawk reached underneath her sweater with his left hand.

Pulling down the top of her bra, he sought out her nipple. She had these small, peach-sized numbers he wanted to pop into his mouth.

Lexi had the kind of tits that looked great braless in sweaters and even better with summer dresses. He thumbed her nipples until they pebbled. Impatient to be inside of her, he curbed the urge to lick, kiss and possess every part of this woman. Hell, maybe he should take his time? She might never let him do this again.

What the hell is that? Hawk had to shove that negative shit out of his mind. He was Hawthorne Maze. Regardless of her sexy genius status, he was a freaking star.

"Mmm-m," she moaned.

Inching his hand up her thigh, Hawk damn near destroyed the lacy thong barrier that separated him from his goal. He yanked at the side and tried to pull them down. Usually he had more finesse, but he couldn't control his frantic need. Thankfully, Lexi tilted her hips up, which helped him pull the thin fabric the rest of the way off.

Anticipating one another, they moved together in a sensual dance. She unbuttoned his jeans and shoved them down while he sucked on her neck. Palming her slick pussy within his hand, Hawk placed his tongue against her smooth chocolate skin and inhaled her sweet taste into his mouth.

"Mmm-m," she moaned again. He rubbed his thumb over her taut clit while D'Angelo's *Brown Sugar* streamed from his phone.

Hawk lifted his head to meet her luscious lips and attack her beautifully kissable mouth. Lexi gave a healthy tug to his shaft, forcing his insides to jump. Biting down on her lower lip, Hawk surged forward and bucked into her warm, wet slit.

"Shit," he hissed while slipping his hand across her breast to grab her lovely neck. Hawk rolled his hips and thrusted deeper into her.

"Ahh-h," she mewed.

Tightening his grip on her throat, he pumped his cock with controlled strokes. As he ground into her pussy, she dropped her head back, muttering words he couldn't decipher. She was soft and feminine, and he took comfort in her body. Anchoring her neck within his grip, he fucked Lexi limp.

A sweet hitch in her breath signaled for him to increase his pace.

"Fu-uck!" she cried.

Before Hawk released his load inside of her, a burst of colored swirls of emotion rendered him blind. His heart seemed to stutter in his chest. He leaned over the beauty, fighting to catch his breath.

"Whoo-o." Lexi wiggled from beneath him. Damn near drained to a point of fatigue, Hawk fell on to the table. Balancing himself precariously with his forearm across the wood surface, he fought to get his heart rate back to normal.

"That was…" Lexi adjusted her bra.

Hawk attempted to bring himself back to the land of the living by meditating his way out of a fatal heart attack.

"I mean, I really…" Lexi kicked her panties off the tip of her boot and caught them in one hand. "Man. So…" A pretty blush of red flushed the rounds of her brown cheeks. She turned toward the window behind her, then faced him again. "It looks like it's coming down hard," she rushed out. "You better get going."

"Whooa, what?" With his cock hanging out, he sat up.

"How bad would it look for the Northern Night Enforcer to get in a car accident coming from a bar?" Lexi said.

"Royals," he muttered, suddenly feeling like a groupie. "Uh, well, I'm from Canada and—"

"That door sticks like crazy," she chirped.

Hawk couldn't quite put his finger on her sudden hyper demeanor. *Jazzed, geeked out*? He didn't know what to call it, but he was confused. Pushing his cock back into his jeans, he zipped himself up as Lexi smoothed out her skirt.

"So, slam it real hard on your way out."

"Huh?"

"The door." She stepped closer and planted a kiss on the corner of his mouth. "Thanks for that, I really needed it."

In all the days of his slutty, skirt-chasing life, this had never happened to him. Feeling worse than a discarded tissue in Las Vegas, he moved his mouth, to tell her exactly what he thought about it. However, no words came out. He tried to say goodnight, but she'd already crossed the bar and pushed the kitchen door open.

"What the fuck was that?" he asked no one but himself.

Chapter Eleven

The last bit of sunlight shone through his floor-to-ceiling window. It was that weird time of year where it got dark early, but it wasn't time for daylight savings quite yet.

After he had his hot but weird-ass encounter with Lexi, he'd gone home and vegged in front of the TV. Old Bruce Lee movies played back-to-back and he got lost in the wonderful world of martial arts. Anything had been better than dwelling. He felt worse than a used condom.

Clad in nothing but a towel, he idly considered where the hell he'd left his robe. He loved the big, plush ones. On more than five occasions, his past sleepover guests had snuck straight out of the door with them. Hawk snorted. Tiny girls with big purses couldn't be trusted.

As the sound of his phone chimed, Hawk grabbed the coffee mug from under the Nespresso machine and groggily made his way to the bathroom.

Too early in the morning for anybody other than someone who had kids, he hit the accept button to FaceTime with Knox. "Big dog! What'cha got planned for later?" Knox's enormous head filled his tablet screen that leaned against the bathroom mirror.

"Why? What are you trying to rope me into?" Hawk smirked at his best friend. After taking a sip of from the rich coffee, he set the mug down and reached for his shaving cream. When Knox didn't answer, he decided to speed the conversation along. "Marketing event at NikeTown."

"Coming to Moe's later?"

Not if my head was on fire and Moe's is the last place on Earth that had water. "Maybe," he lied. "But I have this thing with the team. Some get-together one of the bigwigs is throwing."

"Okay, what's up? You never go to shit like that."

Hawk avoided any and all eye contact and lathered his face with shaving cream. "Nothing. I feel like I should put in a little face time," he muttered.

"Are you avoiding something...or, better yet, someone?"

Hawk dried his hand on his washcloth before he grabbed the razor off the sink.

"Don't know what you're talking about," he said, knowing full well what he meant. Knox could read him better than a football playbook, and that's why he decided to keep his eyes trained on the mirror and tighten up the edges of his stubble. The grizzly bear transformation didn't appeal to him. The first year most the rookies attempted to rock that crazy lumberjack look, but most of them hadn't even hit puberty.

"Right." Knox sighed. "Look... Moe's is having an amateur night, and a couple of A&R reps from record companies are supposed to be there. We thought it would be cool to support the bar, and since you're off tonight—"

"Yeah, I'm going to have to pass." Hiring a barber would be a lot less time-consuming, but Hawk had learned to do everything for himself. To rely on others never seemed to work out.

"How about you—?"

"No." He turned to face Knox head-on. "I'm not watching the girls."

Once his best friend's huge smile widened to the point it damn near took up the entire tablet, Hawk knew he had been caught. "Tell me you didn't, bro. Tell me you didn't."

Shit! The guilt must have been written across his face. "Sorry, no babysitting tonight." Hawk hit the side of the sink with the razor, knocking off the hairs.

"Yeah, we're good on that front. I just needed to see that stupid 'what have I done' expression on your face in person."

"Nothing—"

"Happened, right? I got it. You usually call me when you get in town, but not this time." Hawk tilted his head toward the screen to catch Knox's slimy smirk and shrugged. "Let me know if you change your mind about the bar."

"Sure," he muttered, irritated that Knox could get under his skin.

"And, Hawk—"

"Let me say hi to Uncle Hawk. Let me say hi, Daddy."

Hawk waited for the cutest kid to take over her dad's tablet.

"Later, sweetie. Uncle Hawk needs to figure out what he's going to tell Mr. Moe at our next poker game. I mean, 'oops' isn't going to cut it this time."

"Bye," Hawk ground out before he hung up. Considering Knox ran a team of legendary misfits, Hawk found it hard to believe the Maverick's GM had enough time on his hands to mess with him. "Worry about your pregnant wife and your first-rate team of idiots," he remarked far too late.

* * * *

Moe's line went out through the door and around the corner. Lexi helped Simone behind the bar. They had a good rhythm going — throw in the ice, pour, mix, repeat.

Don't forget to smile, but not with too many teeth. One of the regulars had warned her it was a creepy turn-off. Of course, he'd been beyond drunk, but it had seemed truthful enough when she'd helped him into the cab two weeks ago. As the emcee took the stage to kick off the show, Pop's hard, scruffy voice rose above the bar noise. "I've never seen it this crowded before."

"Didn't think you'd make it tonight." Lexi turned around to fist bump her old man. Seriously swamped, she didn't have time to greet him properly. Since Moe had been under the weather, Lexi was happy to see him out and about. The music would do him some good.

"And miss all the fun?" Blues artists were the biggest snobs on the planet. Regardless of the good buzz around all the up-and-comers, they reserved the right to pick the newbies' bones clean.

Lexi had set up a video feed of the stage in the VIP room for the regulars to voice their opinions in peace. Moe tipped his derby cap at them, and Simone threw him a two-finger salute before he moseyed along.

"Need help?" Remy asked, joining them.

"Something tells me if I say no it wouldn't make a bit of difference."

"Probably not." Remy slid behind the bar, going straight to the tap, which was smart. If someone knocked out the beer orders, they could keep the complaints down to a minimum.

"Did your husband manage to put you in time-out like he wanted?"

"He mentioned that?" Remy chuckled.

"Who couldn't use a time-out?" Simone said.

"Came off a little sexist," Lexi admitted.

"It's actually really sweet. Knox books a five-star hotel room. I binge on junk food and Netflix for the rest of the day."

"Please, someone give me a time-out!" Simone cried.

"I'll give you a time-out, baby." A group of guys laughed on the other side of the bar and high-fived each other.

"Hey, hey, hey, this is the era of 'me too' and 'time-outs'." Simone threw Peaches' special lemonade mix in the blender with vodka and turned it on. "You can't say things like that," she screamed over the noise. "For instance, what if a waitress, who will remain nameless, said that a part of your anatomy is not only a tiny boat but a very disappointing motion in her ocean?"

"Ooohh," the dude's group of friends mocked him.

He flicked off Simone, and snatched his drink off the bar. Used to Simone's little zingers, Lexi turned her attention back to Remy.

"But she's basically using kids' terminology for a cute euphemism on his wife."

"True, but my time-out is all about adult hedonisms he can't very well say in front of the kids... You want to get pounded until you're limp, then eat Doritos all night?"

"Now I want a time-out," one of the dudes at the bar whined.

Chapter Twelve

Hawk's Nike event had gone better than he'd expected. A ridiculous amount of fans had shown up to buy his exclusive jersey. Once he'd hawked enough products and charmed his way through the media junkets, he headed to a housewarming party for one of his teammates.

Adrift without an anchor, he stepped into the posh, high-rise condominium. Usually after a huge meet-and-greet, Hawk would go to Moe's. If he hadn't been dismissed outright by Lexi, he would have skipped this bullshit with his teammates entirely. There was no one for him to hang out with, which sounded teenage angsty, but who wanted to deal with this type of shit alone?

"The old man finally showed up!" someone yelled over the harsh, big-room house music. The place was decorated in gaudy-ass neon lights and cheetah prints. He forgot which young'un had moved into the Lake

Shore Drive condo, but figured it was probably the kid's first apartment. The place was hideous.

"Beer, vodka or what is it you senior citizens drink? Martinis shaken, not stirred." The group of losers drunkenly chuckled at their own joke. "Oh, that's right. He doesn't drink —"

"Or have fun," a Swedish rookie finished for their host.

"Surprised the old folks' home let you come out so late." The laughter at his expense grew louder. If there were a moment in the last five years that he needed a drink, he felt tonight qualified.

"Here." The girlfriend to the Russian handed him a drink off a tray. "Virgin Long Island."

"This is basically a Shirley Temple," he said.

"Yeah, but I didn't want it to sound unmanly." She giggled and went back to serving the rest of the room.

Slipping his big frame around the drunken, sweaty bodies, he headed to the next room and took a swig of his drink. The kid's apartment was tacky, but his media room was the worst by far. Burgundy leather couches and awards decorated the living room. Hawk sighed. He didn't want to mope at home alone, and that was the only reason he'd attended this little shindig.

"Hey, man," Marco called out to him. Hawk slapped hands with the Northern Royals latest and most controversial trade. "You usually don't come to these things."

"Try to avoid them, but my night opened up — and you?"

"The coach got onto my ass about 'cultivating relationships'." He held up his fingers into quote marks.

"In other words, he threatened you," Hawk translated for him.

Marco had been in the league a good ten years, but had kept his hard-partying ways a lot longer. For the most part, Hawk didn't really know all that much about his teammate. Still, he managed to get along better with him than the rest of the rest of his co-workers.

"Pretty much. I'm giving this shit another ten minutes, and I suggest you do the same. This mess is for the dumbbells and rookies."

He nodded his head at Marco's assessment, but suddenly felt lightheaded. Crap, he needed to check his blood sugar.

"See you later, man." Hawk patted his shoulder and walked down the connecting hallway, hoping the bathroom was nearby.

* * * *

Customers surrounded the stage. A young, black teenager from the southside commanded everyone's attention. Lexi felt her first amateur contest had gone better than expected.

Lashonda walked into the bar. "Finally made it." She swung her straight, burgundy hair off her shoulder. "And look who I brought with me."

The woman who trailed behind the black Jessica Rabbit waved at everyone. *Shit!* Didn't these chicks have at least one basic-ass friend? *Hell, if I stick around long enough, it might end up being me.*

"Lexi Waters, Dahl Carter," Remy introduced them.

"Hey, that rhymes," the woman who was the color of a perfectly crafted candy apple said. Lexi took her extended hand over the bar and shook it. "I've been dying to meet you! Anyone who can deal with this merry band of lunatics." Dahl reminded her of one of those sex pots from the seventies who had invented slo-mo hair swings and wore one size too small cotton shirts, tight shorts and had a smile that could rival the sun.

"Don't trust anything she says," Remy warned. "This one is trying to butter you up so she can poach Peaches from you."

"And on that note..." Dahl threw a cheeky wink over her shoulder as she beat a path to the kitchen.

Lexi opened her mouth to give a classic retort, but loud cackles near the bar's entrance pulled her attention. Afraid the drunk gang would be a problem, she tried to track down the bar's bouncer that she usually hired for special occasions.

"You don't seem worried." Lashonda plopped down on a stool. "Dahl is hella persuasive." The video vixen was the pure softy of the group. Lexi felt she was getting their personalities down, which slightly worried her. Close friendships had never been her jam.

"Moe and Peaches have some kind of blood oath," she admitted. "I'm not too worried about it."

The obnoxious laughter went up a huge notch. She looked for the muscle she'd hired, but he was nowhere in sight. It was getting late and no one wanted to deal with the drunks.

"Let me," Lashonda offered. "I'm a pro at this."

"This ought to be good," Simone said.

The tall beauty pulled herself up to her full height and went straight for the small group. As she dressed them down, the college-aged children immediately shrank away. Lashonda reached over and snatched the phone out of the girl's hand.

"Not positive, but I think that's illegal," Simone whispered.

In a chastising manner, Lashonda wagged the cell phone at them before something on the screen caught her attention.

"If she gives it back, I don't think it qualifies as a crime," Lexi answered.

The emcee assisted Moe's contest winner off the stage. While most of the crowd migrated closer to the singer who had won the contest, Lashonda approached the bar with the phone facing out. "Hey, is this..."

Lexi set down the mug and hovered close. A few scantily dressed beer girls addressed the live feed. "Let's see how much this big boy can really do!" a platinum blonde screamed before turning her phone toward a half-passed-out Hawk.

"This enforcer may be called to the penalty box, but we'll try one more Brewhouzer Bitters to see if he can hit a goal," another woman with even skimpier clothes suggested.

"How can we find out where he's at?" Remy gestured for the owner of the phone to join them. "You, phone girl, come here." Her tone hardened. The chick's shoulders sagged as she made her way toward them.

"Why? What's going on?" Lexi had to admit she was disappointed, since she honestly couldn't stop thinking about the previous night. Of course, if she were honest with herself, it was a one-and-done type of deal, and she had no room to feel anything, honestly.

"Hawk's diabetic. He doesn't drink."

Lexi's ears pricked at that bit of information.

"Who's this on your friends list?" Remy asked her.

"It's just some social media talk show. These girls from the restaurant, *Jugs*, get invited to high-profile parties and mingle."

Remy rolled her hand for her to get to the point.

"Short-story it," Lashonda rudely told her.

"In other words, I follow her, but I don't have a clue what her location could be."

As the seriousness of the situation seeped in, Lexi grabbed the cell out of Lashonda's hand and memorized the girl's username.

"Remy, pull up this app on your phone," Lexi instructed. She dug into her jean pocket and took it out. "Follow the Jugs girls." She then spouted out three names that were on their inner circle list.

"Dani Lyons is an editor we have in common," Remy said.

"Can you text her and get her to go online?"

"Okay." Her fingers flew across her screen lightning fast. "She's on now. What next?"

Lexi tossed the phone back to the girl Lashonda had stolen it from. "Grab a seat. Drinks are on the house for you and your friends."

"Really?" Delight brightened the girl's whole face.

"Yes, but you have a hundred-dollar cap, so don't get stupid."

"What a way to punish her," Lashonda murmured. The college kids hurried off toward the main floor. "How are we going to find him now?"

Putting her hand out, she waited for Remy to place her cell into her open palm. Lexi quickly reconfigured the GPS settings to track down the Jugs girls. "Got it! Simone, make sure Dahl doesn't steal Peaches" —as she untied her apron and handed it to her bartender, she spouted off a list—"and don't give those kids more than fifty-dollars-worth of our alcohol."

"Water that shit down. Got it." Simone smirked.

Rolling three deep, Lexi was on her way to rescue the man who had given her the best dick she had ever had. *Mixed messages anyone?*

Chapter Thirteen

They had arrived at the luxury condo in a record fifteen minutes. In downtown Chicago traffic on a Friday that was a small miracle. Remy had greased the doorman's hand a good one hundred dollars to get them into the building. They found the condo from the obnoxiously loud music that blared out of the corner apartment. Lashonda banged her fist against the door with the authority of SWAT.

"When are you going to admit to Knox that you're for real pregnant?" Lashonda asked, pounding the door again as Remy leaned against the wall and sighed.

Fanning herself, she shrugged. "He'll figure it out eventually."

Lexi's gaze glided down to Remy's nonexistent baby bump...a burger bump, maybe, but definitely no baby.

"Odds are he already knows," Lashonda muttered.

"Then why should I say anything?"

"Wow, his competitive streak mixed with your stubbornness makes for one big, ball of crazy in the

Bell-Knox household." Lashonda beat on the door with the side of her fist even harder.

"What the hell?" A teenager opened the door. Lexi assumed he was a kid by his baby-fat fresh face and hard Finnish accent. Hawk had mentioned all the rookies were foreigners. "Oh, hey, are you the strippers we ordered? But you're—"

"Say it. I dare you." Lashonda shoved him to the side. "If you want to beat it to a blonde, all you have to do is look in the mirror. Geesh, get a little variety in your life."

"Find the bathroom. I'll meet you there." Remy pulled out a professional camera from her purse and snapped pictures of the kitchen. Lexi opened her mouth but shut it quick enough since she probably didn't want to know what the hell Remy was doing.

Moving through a ton of people, she tried to figure out the layout of the place.

"Do you know where we're going?" Every inch of the condo was taken up with young, drunk bodies.

"Yeah, I've done a shoot in this building before." Lexi had recently learned everyone's profession. Lashonda was one of the top commercial stylists in her field. "This way."

Wonder Woman cut a path for them through the crowd, but Lexi still managed to lose her. Knocked around by the drunk idiots, she rose on her tippy toes to pinpoint the Amazon within the crowd. "Come on, gurl. You run a bar." Lashonda clamped a hand down on her wrist. "Smack some of these babies out of the way." She yanked her into a room. "Whoever owns this place has a shit aesthetic." While the leopard prints begged for a second more satisfying death from the floor, Lexi had a hard time focusing her eyes on any one color in the room.

Across the main bedroom a blue light shone under a closed door. "God, I hope nothing gross is going on in there. I have a nervous stomach," Lashonda admitted. She grabbed the knob and shoved the door open. Perched on top of the toilet lid, a Jugs girl had draped herself onto a half-passed-out Hawk.

Barely able to hold himself upright, he was weaving and his head bobbed back and forth. "Okay, night-night. Fun's over." Lashonda plucked the phone out of one of the girl's hands and pressed a few buttons on the screen before she threw it out of the door.

"Hey!" While the half-dressed woman ran after her cell, Lashonda snatched the other chick off Hawk's lap. "Go help your friend," she suggested, pushing her out of the bathroom.

Lexi hurried to slam it shut behind her. "Where does he keep his insulin?"

"Dre told me one of his pants pockets. He had to shoot him up once."

"Hawk." Lexi smiled. Peeling back his eyelids, she checked to see if his eyes were dilated.

She searched his jacket pockets but came up with nothing "I'm going to feel around for your insulin pen, and —" Lexi moved to his chest, touching his hard pec.

"Ghosted," he murmured before her hand bumped the needle in his front pocket, similar to a decorative pen. She pulled it out. "You ghosted me —"

"A little help, please?" Lexi asked Lashonda while she placed the pen in her mouth to pull the cap off between her teeth. Lashonda leaned him forward and together they pulled off his jacket. Once she got his sleeve unbuttoned, they were able to roll his shirt over his thick arm.

Before she could get the pen out of her mouth, Lashonda rushed past her.

"Where are you going?" she asked, popping off the cap.

"Look... I told you I'm squeamish, and don't for a second think I missed Hawk saying you ghosted him after you banged."

"Huh, that's not what he said." Lexi plucked the bottom of the needle with her index finger.

"No" — Lashonda opened the bathroom door and arched her wildly shaped eyebrow in her direction — "but you banged."

"What's going on?" Remy asked, out of breath. She squeezed into the crack of the door.

"A lot." Lashonda slipped out of the room, leaving them with the big man.

"Ah, the needle." Remy strolled over to the tub and took a seat on the ledge. "She's such a baby."

Lexi searched the middle of his arm for a vein, then tapped it until it bulged. Taking her time, she slipped the sharp tip into his arm and pressed on the plunger.

"Nurse or Fortune 500 owner of a tech company... Who can tell the difference?"

"My mom had diabetes." Lexi pulled the needle out and yanked a square of toilet paper from the roll to hold onto his arm. "It looks like he crashed. Hopefully, he'll be okay in a few minutes, but we should probably call an ambulance, just in case."

"The boys are on their way." Remy tapped on her phone screen. "Besides, he has a private doctor who's going to meet us at my house."

"Oh," Lexi said with a hint of disappointment. She wanted to stay with Hawk but didn't want to intrude on their system. These people were practically family.

"Unless you want to stay with him. I mean, you're awfully good with that needle."

Schooling her expression into an unreadable mask, Lexi lifted her eyes to meet Remy's. "True, that could come in handy."

"And, according to Shonda, you guys banged...so there's that." Remy tilted her head to the side, probably daring her to lie. Instead of digging herself into a bigger hole, Lexi returned her attention back to the patient.

"Who-o did what-t?" he slurred. Hawk attempted to sit up, but Lexi gently pushed him back down.

"Relax, big fella." Hawk's hazel stunners drunkenly glided over the room before landing on her face.

"Hey." He smiled.

"Hey yourself."

As he flipped his palm up, Lexi shyly sucked her lower lip between her teeth and intertwined their fingers together. Closing his eyes, he slumped against the toilet tank again. "Don't go anywhere, okay?"

"Okay," she agreed. Strangely enough, this offbeat night had turned into one of the more romantic ones she'd ever had.

* * * *

The soothing sounds of orchestra violins was the first thing to tickle his nerves. Hawk opened his eyes to a blurred version of his bedroom. He kept blinking until he could see everything in a less abstract way.

Above the fire that roared in the hearth, his gaze connected with the vibrant colors of his Corey

Barksdale oil painting. Jazz musicians played their instruments in wild red and yellow tones. The picture popped among the cool slate blues and grays in the bedroom.

Turning his head to the side, he found Lexi next to the bed, studying her tablet. She sat with her forehead furrowed in deep concentration and her legs tucked underneath her in his Garbo wingback chair. Soft snowflakes drifted to the ground outside the window behind her.

While her dark brown eyes twinkled with amusement, Lexi's lush lips curved at the corners. Appearing even younger than her thirty-two years, she wore her short, black hair slicked away from her makeup-free face, and the pink sweater that dwarfed her petite frame accentuated the color of her pretty brown skin.

Perfect! He damn near sighed out loud.

Blood rushed to his cock, stiffening his already-semi-hard rod. At least the most important thing on him was working properly. The rest of his body felt like he'd been beat with a sack of potatoes. He hadn't felt this bad in years. He was groggy as fuck, and his heart beat wildly in his chest when he realized he had a game to play.

"Oh shit, what day is it?"

Lexi smiled over the top of her tablet. "Saturday."

Panicked, Hawk yanked the sheet from his body and tried to crawl out of bed, but a wall of muscle pain prevented him from going anywhere.

"Whoa there, big fella." She laid her hand on his bare chest and tried to push him back onto his bed. Of course, she couldn't possibly move him. "Doctor prescribed rest. You're out for the night."

"Shit," he hissed. "What did he tell my coach?"

"Dehydration."

"Okay." He nodded in agreement with that excuse. "That's better than the truth, I guess."

Lexi moved from the chair and took a seat on the edge of his bed. Hawk plopped back onto his pillow. "They don't know you have diabetes?"

"Yes, but I've never let it affect my game and I want to keep it that way." They sat quietly listening to the hypnotizing melody of the violins until the song played out. "This music…" He turned his head to the left to get a better view of her.

"Violin Concerto Florence Price. She was the first black woman in America to have her art performed by an orchestra."

"She wasn't on that list of music you sent me."

"That's because you asked for neo-soul and R&B, not classical composers." She chuckled.

How cool can this woman possibly be? Not for the first time, Hawk realized he was crazy comfortable in her presence. There were no awkward silences where he needed to fill the space. Their conversations never felt forced.

Then why the hell did she hit and quit the other night? It was on the tip of his tongue to ask her.

"The doctor thinks someone drugged you. He took a sample of your blood for testing," Lexi told him.

Hawk nodded. He wasn't that close to his teammates, but he hated to think someone on his team was capable of drugging him. "In the meantime, how did you get roped into babysitting duties?"

"We drew straws, and I came up short." Lexi batted her lush lashes, throwing him a hundred-watt smile.

"Thanks for sitting with me. If you need to get back to the bar, I completely understand."

Knox had been his emergency contact since college. Anytime he had an episode, it was either his best friend or Knox's family waiting for him when he came out the other side of it.

"And give up this chilled-out awesomeness?"

They stared at one another. Even though his dick was up for the exercise, he felt it would be pathetic on his part to make a move. She'd nursed his weak ass through the night and there was nothing sexy about boinking the diabetic dude. Of course, he wanted to yank her body to his chest and kiss those pretty lips, but he couldn't imagine first base with a sickie was at all sexy.

"In that case…" Hawk reached for the remote that was Velcroed to the side of his nightstand and pressed a button. The TV slowly descended from the ceiling at the foot of the bed. "Pick your poison."

"Oh, I was wondering where you were hiding that." To his delight, she snuggled in next to him, plucking the remote from his hand. "We're going to watch something mind numbing, then we'll take a break to grab food that a Michelin-star chef left for us."

"Dahl cooked!" Happier than a kid on Christmas, he wanted to run into the kitchen and check out what she'd made. However, Lexi felt entirely too good cozied up to his side for him to chance moving away from her.

He had never whined about his disease. It was one more challenge he'd overcome. Whether he felt like shit or not, he always made it to game day. Oh well, there was a first time for everything.

Taking full advantage of his sick day, Hawk leaned his head against her peach-sized breasts and settled back.

Chapter Fourteen

California's weather went from hot to less hot in four short seasons. Winters consisted of drizzle or mudslides with absolutely *no* in between. Often Lexi had felt the amount of sun-to-cloud ratio threw off everyone's natural serotonin levels.

The second her plane touched down at LAX's tarmac, she was on edge.

SugarTech's board had filed for an emergency deposition.

Due to bumper-to-bumper traffic, her attorney had the opportunity to brief her on the hearing. She planned on visiting the West Coast for less than twenty-four hours, and even that seemed too long. The only bright light in this whole mess was Hawk. They were in the same city, and he wanted to take her out. It was the one thing that made her visit the least bit tolerable.

"Why?" Lexi stood in the hotel check-in line. Cradling the phone, she dug into her purse for her wallet.

"Excuse me?" Maureen said.

"We have gone over where to meet, what to say and not to say, but you haven't told me why I'm back in Sunnydale."

"Sunny what?" Maureen repeated.

"It's the hellmouth, or fu-u—" Lexi caught herself before she lost her shit. "Why am I here?" The boutique hotel did nothing to suppress her mounting nerves. Trendy spiked chandeliers hung above her head. White fluffy fur was placed on every available chair. She would have found the place cute if she didn't have to waste the little bit of money she had made at Moe's to book a room.

"They're claiming you're in violation of the morality agreement."

Images of the sex video immediately flashed in her mind before her she found her wallet. "For example?"

"The incident happened on November fifth. That's all the information I have."

As she stepped up to the front desk, she sighed in relief. Josh had sent that video over the summer, which means it probably wasn't the problem. She gave her name to the front desk agent. "Hi, Lexington Waters."

"Does that ring a bell?" Maureen pushed.

Lexi slid her credit card across the counter and tried to remember what, if any significance that date held.

"Not really." Lexi accepted her credit card and key from front desk before she made her way to the elevators. Nabbing an empty cab, she stepped in.

"We're nearing the quarterly meeting for the board, and we don't need one of your transgressions used against us."

One of? Ye of little faith. She pouted at her lawyer and hit the button for the upper level.

Barely listening to the woman after that insult, Lexi waited for the elevator to take her to the fifth floor. "If you can think of anything, let me know. I don't like surprises."

The doors opened and she stepped out.

As Lexi headed down the hall, she ran through anything that could have possibly forced her back to the West Coast. Josh wanted to financially bleed her dry, but his ultimate goal was majority ownership of the company. In other words, he needed to break her.

Lexi arrived at her hotel room and slid her key card into the slot. "Trust me. You'll be the first to know." She ended the call without another word and opened her door to white fufu décor.

It wasn't exactly the Beverly Wilshire, where Josh had thrown their last Christmas party. Of course, Lexi wouldn't know anything about that since she'd been banned at least one hundred feet from the company. A few of SugarTech's associates had posted the gathering on social media. Judging from the photos, the employees had had one hell of a night.

Nevertheless, her hotel room was contemporary, bright and for lack of a better term, nice. Drawn to the big box that sat on top of the queen-sized bed, she picked up the card placed under the red bow.

Trust us. He'll love it.
The Wives

She explained her visit to the West Coast as work stuff... Hopefully they had believed her.

Lexi tossed the card and yanked the top off. Removing the tissue paper, she uncovered a sexy ensemble that she would have never worn in a million years.

Running late for her date, Lexi hurried into the elevator cab and pressed the big L button. She switched her phone to her other hand and flipped her cape over her shoulder.

"Wait! Let me see it again?" Dahl said.

Once she'd finished getting dressed, Lexi had called the wives for their stamp of approval. Lashonda had included instructions on how to style her hair. Holding the phone above her head, she checked her makeup.

"Those little curls are perfect with that outfit," Dahl cooed.

"Puhleese! I'm a freakin' professional," Lashonda yelled somewhere behind her. Every month the wives got together for a girls' night. Lexi hadn't had the chance to attend, but she promised them once her schedule opened up, she'd be there with bells on. "Hawk's going to love it—"

"Wait a minute. What does this outfit have to do with—"

Dahl handed the phone off before Lexi could finish her question.

Remy's smiling face came into focus as she bounced her baby on her hip. "Wow, you look great."

"Thanks. Uh..." She switched gears, not knowing how to approach the next topic without giving too much about the mess that was her life away. "That night with Hawk at that party, do you remember anything that might be incriminating?"

"Hmm-m." While Remy glanced over her shoulder, the baby tried to reach for the screen. She moved away from the room the wives were in. "Does this have anything to do with SugarTech?" Not totally surprised the award-winning journalist knew about her legal drama, she nodded her head. "Who's your attorney?"

"Maureen Wendt."

"And your—"

"Depo is tomorrow," Lexi told her. The lights on top of the elevator flashed quickly to each floor.

"Okay, got it. Don't worry about this stuff. Go out and have fun."

"But—"

"And Shonda's right… Hawk's going to go crazy when he sees you. Leave the cape on until you get to the restaurant, okay?"

"Seriously, what is the deal with this outfit?"

The elevator doors slid open. Lexi stepped into the bustling lobby. Apparently, her hotel turned into a major pick-up spot during the evening hours.

"Tell Ms. Lexi bye, sweetie."

The baby, who was busy eating her mom's hair, used her free hand to enthusiastically wave at the screen.

"Bye, cutie." She blew her a kiss before hanging up.

"It's good to see you're not holding a grudge." Lexi jerked away from the sound of his slight New England accent. "You look good, M&M."

Josh's use of her old college nickname ignited a flame of hate in the pit of her stomach. "What do *you* want?"

"Hey, I come in peace." With a good-humored smile, he held up his hands with his fingers split in the Doctor Spock's Trekkie salute. Even though he was well out of his twenties, he still held onto his tech bro arrogance like a badge of honor. "Let's go to the bar." He placed his hand on her shoulder to guide her across the room. "We need to catch up."

It was a lighthearted request that in no way came off in a menacing manner, but Lexi knew better. As rage created an acidic coat in her throat, mimicking a bout of bad indigestion, she slipped away from his touch.

"According to the restraining order I have to stay at least one hundred feet away from you. Catching up over drinks doesn't seem like a viable reason to visit county lockup...again."

Josh's smile broadened, stretching the skin on his angular face tighter. "Don't make this harder than it has to be, Lex."

"Sorry... I no longer have time for this special edition of Josh Stewart throws a rock and hides his hand."

Wary of his presence in general, Lexi stepped around him and caught a glimpse of hope. Hawk stood outside the hotel's huge front window, signing autographs. A large crowd had formed around the professional hockey player. The sight of him loosened the strong grip of hate that burned in her chest.

"Quit dragging this shit out," Josh said in her ear. "This will be much easier on the both of us if you give me majority share."

"Fuck off," she tossed over her shoulder. No longer interested in anything he had to say, Lexi walked away from her miserable ex.

"Don't you dare ignore me." Josh grabbed her by the arm, jerking her around to face him. "It will be in your best interest to hand over those shares."

That creepy smile hadn't slipped an inch. *What the hell did I ever see in him?* "Let me go or I will embarrass the shit out of you," she said, snatching her arm away. Everything in Lexi told her to run from the narcissistic freak, but she wouldn't give him the satisfaction.

Instead, she slowly strolled through the busy lobby, cheekily showing off Lashonda's lovely outfit.

Without glancing back, she maneuvered her way between the lobby full of guests. Since the crowd around Hawk had thinned, she didn't feel as if she were intruding upon the hockey player's moments with his fans. The bellhop opened the door, allowing the toasty California air to blanket her.

Chapter Fifteen

Attraction was one thing, but a deep-down *like* for someone was the good stuff. It warmed the blood not only by touch but sight. Hawk hadn't been this much in *like* with someone since high school.

In ninth grade, he'd pretended he needed tutoring in college prep calculus. Amy Brookes had seemed reluctant to help, but he'd managed to crack the nerdy cute girl code. They got along great and even managed to make out a few times before she'd totally decimated his heart. Sweet, dear Amy had wanted an introduction to their football team's infamous quarterback, Gavin Knox. It wasn't the first time that had happened, but it had definitely been the most impressionable.

Scanning the trendy, American-Korean-fusion restaurant, Hawk waited for his date at their VIP table. He hadn't thought about that in years, but when he'd picked Lexi up from the hotel, he had caught sight of her with some guy. From the outside looking in, the pair's conversation seemed intense. Since Hawk had gotten well acquainted with that manicured, douchey type of jerk growing up, watching Lexi's body language had told him something was off.

As he waited for her to return from the restroom by skimming the menu, Hawk twisted his silver wolf ring around his thumb. More nervous than he'd ever been on a date, he wondered what the hell was wrong with him.

"There's never a line to the men's room — or is that inconvenience reserved just for women?"

Hawk slid his gaze from her sexy heels up her sleek legs. A narrow black skirt covered her knees. Hawk wanted to push the tight fabric up her thighs to see the color of her panties.

"Uh...who? Uh..." Losing his train of thought, he reached for the glass of unsweetened tea. At one point in time, the top she wore may have been a man's white tuxedo vest, but she had it fashioned into a form-fitting halter.

Thankfully, Lexi took her seat before he decided to act on an animal instinct to whisk her out of the restaurant and fuck her in the alley. Since that one indecent night in the bar, they had exhibited the model employer-employee relationship. No blurred lines or touchy-feely stuff in the slightest, but the sight of her brought that ravenous feeling back.

Lexington Waters was not the type to bang in the street — not that there was anything wrong with that. Hockey groupies often eased the burden of the road in an awesome, therapeutic way. However, dirty dumpster sex didn't seem appropriate for this. She had Audrey Hepburn-type beauty, but her outfit told him that maybe somewhere down the road it could be a possibility.

"Are you a fan of the movie *Flashdance*?" he asked.

"Never seen it." She reached for the basket of eggroll breadsticks.

He tried not to stare at her glossy, red-painted lips. Diverting his attention back to her brown eyes, he felt suddenly antsy. He probably shouldn't have worn designer jeans and denim shirt to such a fancy restaurant, but he refused to be anyone else but himself. Unfortunately, fidgeting wasn't an option. This bizarre, out-of-body feeling had more to do with Lexi than his surroundings. He wanted to impress her and didn't have the foggiest idea how to accomplish that insurmountable task.

"It's one of my favorite movies," he confessed. "Back at the boarding school, we only had eighties-anything to watch, and—"

"Wasn't that considered a musical?"

"It was more one long music video that had a motion picture running time," Hawk informed her.

"In other words, perfect 'tween porn."

"A gateway drug, I'm afraid." He reached across the table and used his thumb to wipe the crumbs from the corner of her mouth. Fuck, he wanted to kiss those lips.

"Thanks," she chuckled. While Hawk caressed her slim fingers, he was reluctant to let her go, but he slowly pulled away from her touch.

"Anyway"—he leaned back in his seat, not trusting himself this close to her—"there is a pivotal scene in the movie where Alex, the iron wielder by day, dancer by night—"

"Oh, versatile." She opened her doe eyes wide in a serious, shocked expression.

"No judging," he scolded. Lexi held up her hands in peace before she made a grab for her glass of wine.

"At a fancy restaurant, the lead...correction, the *hot* lead—"

She threw him a cheeky wink before she drank her red wine.

Taking her gesture as a sign of encouragement, he continued. "Alex took off her suit jacket to reveal a cummerbund and a bow tie underneath."

Choking back a laugh, she covered her mouth with her hand. "No shit?" Lexi muttered, once she'd swallowed.

"Apparently you have on the modern version of that outfit." Hawk took in the whole beautiful picture Lexi presented. Her short hair had been slicked away from her face with little ringlets, which accentuated her warm glow. The halter top she wore hugged her sweet breasts perfectly, not to mention the ridiculous amount of skin she displayed. The sight of Lexington Waters created an uncomfortable tightness in the crotch of his jeans.

"Well, it appears the wives are trying their hand at matchmaking," Lexi said, dabbing a bit of wine from her lips. "Is that a good thing?"

The football wives had never bothered to pay attention to his love life before. Of course, no one had ever stuck around long enough, but an endorsement of this magnitude was huge.

"Do you have a minute after dinner?" Hawk asked. He wanted her all damn night, but he had a very short amount of time off.

"Don't you have school tomorrow?" An angelic smile graced her face. The waiter picked that moment to block Hawk's view of her, when he placed their food onto the table.

He waited for their food to be served. "There's something I want to show you."

"Are you sure? I don't want to be a…what do they call it a curse or a bad luck charm for the game tomorrow?" Leaning forward on the table, Lexi put her chin in her hand. This slight shift allowed a good amount of side boob to pop out of her white top.

Yes, he could have a whole dinner date without wanting to take her to bed. Yes, he'd done it before, but it had more to do with the lack of chemistry than anything else. Yes, he absolutely wanted to spend the night with Lexi. However, he had a plane to catch in a few hours for the career that he'd fought his whole life for. In other words, Lexington Waters made him nervous. Hawk took a deep breath and threw everything he knew out of the window.

"First off, that curse shit is reserved for baseball and football. Us hockey players are made of harder stock." Satisfied at the musical, hard belly laugh he'd earned, he sat back and admired the work of art in front of him. "Second, I promise this won't take long."

* * * *

After he'd been dumped on the steps of a church, very few things had been consistent in his life. No one had wanted to adopt the half-Black mutt. The best he could have hoped for was an orphanage bid instead of the foster home bounce around that most of the unwanted kids received. Besides meeting the infamous Gavin Knox, the one thing that had never changed for Hawk was the ice.

The arena was his sanctuary.

While Drake's *Nice For What* blared over the arena's sound system from his cell phone, Hawk sailed around Lexi on the freshly cleaned ice.

"How you doing?" He made a sharp turn, skated toward her at breakneck speed and waved at the custodians who had let them into Lockton University's ice skating rink.

"Amazed at the graceful ass polar bear trying to kill me." Big puffs of air escaped her mouth. Shavings of ice flew off to the side of his skates as he glided to a stop in front of her.

"Hey." He laughed at Lexi. The coat the maintenance man had let her borrow dwarfed her slender frame.

"Full disclosure... I don't know how to ice skate." Since it took a ridiculous amount of coaching to get her onto the ice, he wasn't the least bit surprised.

"From where I'm standing, you look like a pro."

"What the hell made you do this for a living? I mean hello...football?" she asked.

He held her hands and skated slowly backward. Worse than a toddler, Lexi fumbled along.

"Wow, you sound like Dre — and trust me, that's not a compliment."

Lexi snorted out a laugh. "It seems like the same amount of risk factors minus the lethal death blades I'm trying to balance on."

First-time adult skaters usually fought with fists and elbows not to go out onto the ice. Hawk was amazed that she at least gave it a shot. "Hockey careers may cost the players a tooth or —"

"An eye?" she offered.

"But there's far less risk involved. The damage on the body is minimal compared to the NFL." Keeping a tight hold onto her hands, he did a small turn. Lexi stumbled over her skates, but he didn't let her fall. There was no way he could.

"Not to call bullshit on the risk stats, but that doesn't sound like a good reason."

"In Canada, you come out of the womb playing hockey. I had to be bigger, better and faster than everyone else to even make it on my junior high team."

"Because..."

"Seriously, did Dre give you a set of questions to ask me?" He glided to a stop and held her steady. "I'm black and an orphan. Hockey wasn't cheap. I had to be the best to even be considered worthy of charity. Hand-me-down skates and equipment were part of my life for a long time." Immersed into silence from the sudden absence of music, they stared at one another until Miguel's *Simple Things* filled the air.

"Is it worth it?" she asked.

Lost in the way her delicate features made her appear closer to a magical fairy than manager of a blues bar, he missed her question.

"Huh?"

"Being a Black male figure skater with a hockey stick... Is it worth it?"

Refusing to let her off the hook, he pierced her with the classic raised eyebrow, his signature move in a game. His opponent often didn't know what happened after he hit them with the brow.

"Okay, that one I did get from Dre," Lexi confessed with a chuckle.

He slipped his hands under her arms and lifted her. Nose to nose with her, Hawk gazed into her beautiful brown eyes, amber flakes mingling with the darker tones.

"Relax," he told her.

"The ice dancer remark was just a joke." She pouted.

Incapable of holding back any longer, Hawk brought Lexi's lips to his and delivered her a deep, penetrating kiss. She opened her mouth slightly to allow the hot heat of her tongue to meld against his.

As he glided on the ice with the beauty in his arms, he doubled down on his belief that his crush was not only better than attraction but kicked the shit out of his hot-ass lust for Lexington Waters any day of the week.

Chapter Sixteen

Lexi was no longer used to early morning appointments. She hadn't answered emails from SugarTech for months. Whatever bugs that had found their way onto their apps or codes that needed small tweaks were no longer her problem. At Moe's, her life consisted of last calls that far exceeded two a.m. closing times and barely a noon wake-up time.

Summoned to the law offices of Cooper and Shields first thing in the morning, she'd stopped at the local coffee house. The law firm SugarTech had hired already claimed the home field advantage. Why should she allow them to waterboard her with shitty beverages on top of that?

Lexi entered the high rise building five minutes to the hour and stepped off the elevator close to a minute past. Ten seconds late at the most, she opened the door.

"Practically on time," she cheered at her lawyer, Maureen, who met her in the lobby.

"Almost isn't good enough," Maureen shot back.

Resisting the urge to cuss her out, Lexi held up an extra cup of coffee.

"Humph," Maureen grunted, accepting her peace offering. "Quick question." She turned on her heels and walked toward the conference room. "Did we make friends in Chicago?"

"Excuse me?"

Maureen narrowed her unreadable dark eyes at her, then shook her head. "Respond to questions with a yes or a no. Do not expound unless asked and try to keep that vague. Okay?" She stared her down with an icy glare.

Why the fuck did I hire this woman?

"Okay," Lexi responded through clenched teeth. She stepped past her into the empty room and took a seat across from the window. At least she would have something to look at when she mentally tapped out.

Opposing council piled in, slowly filling every available seat. Six against two didn't seem fair, but what did Lexi know? She was merely a developer... *Correction, bartender.* Everyone waited for the stenographer to take her place in the back of the room.

SugarTech's lead council beamed at them. "Good morning, ladies."

Maureen didn't utter a single word. Instead, her lawyer stared death rays, while she robotically sipped her coffee. Unsure what the hell was happening, Lexi remained silent.

"Information has come to our attention that your client violated her morality agreement with SugarTech. Thankfully for her sake, SugarTech decided to be generous and would like to offer Ms. Waters a hefty severance package."

"For her own company," Maureen snorted. "I would think not."

"The evidence we have compiled to submit to the judge will—"

"My client didn't travel over two thousand miles to put any faith into you or your clients. Please"—she twirled her index finger in a bored fashion for him to continue—"present the evidence."

"Fine…" The slick lawyer her ex-husband had hired to represent SugarTech reached across the table and pushed a button on the phone in front of him. Uncharacteristically nervous, Lexi crossed her legs at the calf and fidgeted with her cup lid.

"How are you enjoying our weather? I bet it beats those Midwest storms," opposing council asked with a cheesy grin.

Lexi opened her mouth, but Maureen huffed out a heavy sigh, speaking volumes without actual words.

Moments later, the secretary led a super familiar looking woman into the conference room. Jugs girl number one stepped into the office with the smuggest expression on her overly made-up face. *Someone is an obvious graduate of clown college.* Lexi chuckled at her dig, quickly masking her fumble behind a fake cough.

"State your name for the record," Mr. Reichlen said.

After Juggy number one made sure she was the focus of everyone's attention, she sat up straight with her ginormous boobs pushed out. "Dawn Sweeten," she cooed.

"Please recall the events of November fifth in Chicago, Illinois."

Lexi shifted uncomfortably in her seat.

"Sure, me and my team—"

"Team?" SugarTech's lawyer asked.

"A group of five woman who go out to bars, parties and conventions to supply Juggermeir beers at events. On the night of November fifth, this woman"—she pointed her finger at Lexi—"and her gang ripped my phone out of my hand and stole it."

"That's a violation of Ms. Waters' probation." Mr. Reichlin grinned.

"Interesting." Maureen flipped through a folder in front of her. "Miss—"

"Sweeten," the Jugs girl gleefully provided.

"Was this event you attended scheduled through JMeister Enterprises, Ms. Sweeten?"

"Excuse me?"

"Did Juggermeir beer send you to a Mr. Larsson's event to promote their product?"

"Uh..." The boob girl turned her head toward SugarTech's lawyer. For the briefest of moments, the man closed his eyes before he nodded for her to answer. "It wasn't booked through the promotions manager, if that's what you're asking." She petered off to a thin whisper.

"Well, according to the JMeister's Enterprises, their sales staff can only attend events authorized by their corporate office." Maureen put her finger on the top sheet of paper from the folder and slid it across the glass table. "Any appearance made by Jugs girls wearing the uniform or supplying alcohol to minors is a terminable offense that can also be punishable by a fine and or imprisonment."

As Lexi's lawyer ran down all the ways tits-big-boobies was screwed, all the color drained from her face.

"Now, if you would like to recount the night of November fifth from the minute you entered eighteen-year-old Mr. Larsson's condo..."

Maureen took out a pen and clicked it off and on off with a delirious, psychotic giddiness.

"I, uh...I, uh..." Instead of recalling that evening's events, Ms. Sweeten stumbled over her words, "I don't remember, actually."

The SugarTech's lawyer uncomfortably cleared his throat and pushed away from the table. "Let's take a five-minute break." He stood up. Everyone followed him to the door. "Hey, you." He snapped at the beer girl, then hitched his thumb outside of the room. "Let's go."

The Jugs idiot jerked at the reprimand before rising from her seat and following him. SugarTech's lawyer shut the door, only leaving the stenographer, Maureen and Lexi alone. Super confused, she kept her mouth closed.

They sat in silence until the opposing council minus one Jugs girl returned.

"Where were we?" Mr. Reichlin pulled back his chair with a smile.

"Triple G implants was telling us how you wasted our time coming here."

SugarTech's lawyer arrogantly flipped his tie with a chuckle. "Don't worry, Ms. Wendt, your client has supplied us with ample material. Screen, please." A television dropped down from the ceiling.

"Fancy," Lexi muttered as another familiar face filled the screen and waved.

"Hello! Hi," the college girl greeted them.

"Dammit," Lexi muttered under her breath.

"This is Aimee Shaw. She was unable to fly into the city this afternoon. We'll be using video phone for the deposition," Mr. Reichlin explained. "Thank you for your time, Ms. Shaw. On the night of November fifth, you gathered at Moe's Blues Bar and had your phone stolen by one Lexington Waters."

"By who?" The sober college student seemed even more ditzy than she had on the night in question. Lexi cleared her throat to hide her chuckle behind her hand.

"The manager of the bar…" Mr. Reichlin waited for the girl to reply. "In this room, the manager who stole your phone and used it without your permission."

"Sorry." She squinted closer to her computer screen. "I don't see her."

Dropping his head back, Mr. Reichlin drew a deep breath. "Please take another look, Ms. Shaw."

"Asked and answered," her lawyer sang.

"No, Meghan the Stallion's the one who stole my phone. She had red hair, yay tall." She held her hand over her head. "Really cool. She gave us free drinks and everything, but I don't see her."

With dramatic flair, Maureen slammed her folder shut. "This has been terribly fun." She reached down and grabbed her purse. "Ms. Waters."

Lexi quickly gathered her belongings. Hurrying out of the conference room, she passed the office cubicles, practically running to catch up with Maureen, who had already made it into the elevators.

As the doors were closing, Lexi shoved her hand in the slit, forcing them back open. *Did the bitch roll her eyes?* Taking her place beside her, Maureen stabbed the lobby button over and over until the doors slid shut.

Nervously tapping her foot up and down, Lexi didn't want the awkward silence to overwhelm her but she refused to speak first. Ever since childhood, pregnant pauses filled with fucked-up energy resulted in crazy shit flying out of her mouth.

When the elevator stopped and the doors opened, she followed Maureen out of the cab, crossing the shiny, tiled floor alongside her. *How much money am I paying for this woman to ignore me?*

"They have nothing on you, which means your position at SugarTech is solid," Maureen said, digging into her purse.

"Is that what you got from that?" They stopped in front of her lawyer's overpriced car while she pulled her keys out.

"My professional opinion is they have doo-doo, crap, nada, which means all you have to do is stay out of trouble for more than five minutes." She pressed her car alarm, then opened her door. "Or at least until your next court date...then we'll go after your board." Without a decent exchange of pleasantries or even a measly goodbye, Maureen hopped into her car and slammed the door shut in Lexi's face.

Chapter Seventeen

All those hard-earned, warm fuzzies that had come with her much-needed victory dissipated faster than those frigid Chicago vapors could freeze the dirt in the air.

Snow, snow and more snow greeted her in Chicago. It should have been her first hint of the bad previews to come. Los Angeles may not have offered her much, but it certainly hadn't supplied her with fat snowflakes that drifted from the sky, changing the trajectory of her day.

Lexi's plane touched down to craptastic weather shortly past noon. Since travel had been at a crawl, it took over an hour for her to get to Moe's.

She stood in the midst of a worse shit storm than the one raging outside. Moe's automatic patio window she'd installed last summer was shattered into tiny little pieces on the wood floor.

"It looks like there was some glitch," the fireman screamed over the high-pitched wail of the alarm. "But check around to see if anything's missing."

"The sprinklers went off in the supply room but nowhere else," Simone told him. Lexi's phone rang in her coat, cutting off her answer. She'd switched the whole system over in the bar, except for the storage room.

Apparently, her win in California hadn't flipped her luck toward the better. The minute she'd stepped through Moe's door and comprehended the damage, a swampy fog took over in her head. Lexi dug in her pocket for her phone. Even though her brain begged her to disappear into her shitty apartment to get drunk off old *Dr. Who* episodes and pizza, she continued the very painful act of adulting.

"Hello." A glass of merlot obviously was too much to ask.

"Hey, I need a favor." Hawk's husky voice sliced through the thunder of hate working its way into her soul. It had been a while since she'd encountered this type of rage. The last time she allowed it to take hold, she had gone to jail.

"Okay," Lexi said with an even tone, making sure to keep the crazy-person quiver down to a minimum. "What's up?"

"It will be a couple of days before I can get home, and the kid I use to water my plants is unavailable."

Lexi spun slowly on her heels and headed for the big hole in the window. One of the busboys had mopped the sludge from the incoming snow while her waiter tried to cover the damage with a wood board.

As the strange circus of stupid went on in the bar, several of the regulars huddled across the street.

"Hold a sec, Hawk. Excuse me?" she called out to the fireman who seemed to be doing more flirting with Simone than investigating. "Can we use the kitchen?"

He nodded tersely before turning his attention back to her bartender. "If I recall correctly, you don't have any plants." Using her back, she shoved the swinging door open.

"Maybe you didn't see them," he chuckled, throaty and low.

"Let me guess… You heard about the alarm glitch?" Lexi threw up quotation marks with her mind since her hands couldn't manage it at the moment.

"Glitch?" His voice went up. "What happened?"

Lexi smirked. If nothing else, this man was a sweetheart. "Okay, we'll pretend no one called and told you that my front window is broken and my alarm has gone haywire. What makes you think I'm going to stay at your house?" Placing her hand on Peaches' shoulder, she requested a pot of the woman's famous hot chocolate. Since everything Moe's chef made was awesome, Lexi decided to put famous in front of everything the woman created.

"Sure thing, honeybee."

Eternally grateful that Peaches had stayed on at Moe's well past her retirement date, she kissed the cook's pretty, round cheek and went back to the main room.

"To be clear" — she pushed the swinging door open and crossed the bar — "I don't need charity, and I most certainly don't need to be saved." Lexi had fallen for that bag of tricks once before and she wouldn't do it again — not by any man, but mainly not this sexy mutha fucka.

"The thought never crossed my mind," he purred in her ear. "I merely want my plants to still be alive when I get home, and honestly, you're the most responsible person I know."

"Wow, that's a bald-faced lie if I've ever heard one." Lexi stood in front of Moe's front door. The furious snowflakes that had made her afternoon that much harder to deal with had finally petered out. "Off the top of my head, I can count three of your closest friends who could do a better job than me." She tapped on the glass pane and signaled for the regulars to join her. They stepped off the stoop across the street then hurried toward the bar.

"Hey, we're not done here yet," one of the firemen barked. They were checking out the sprinkler system in the other rooms.

"Don't worry. They won't be in the way."

"If that's the case, please invite the whole block to traipse all over the place." He threw his hands in the air with an exaggerated sigh. "We need to figure out if someone hacked your system initially."

Lexi went to the alarm panel and bypassed the system's code to take it offline. The high-pitched squealing abruptly stopped.

"A glitch, right?" Lexi easily lied. She knew well enough that this personal attack had nothing to do with teenagers running amuck. Josh was written all over it. He wouldn't stop until he got what he wanted — the company...or something much worse. Moe's bar would have sustained astronomical damage had she not updated all the alarm and sprinkler systems earlier this year.

The bell above the door interrupted the racing thoughts in her mind about Josh's next move. "Finally!" Big Al shouted. "I thought we'd freeze our asses off, and trust me, I got a lot of ass to burn through."

Turning away from the fireman, she waved the regular to the back of the bar. She'd have the waitstaff set out the indoor heaters. "Peaches is making hot chocolate. I'll bring it to you guys in a minute."

Cheers of gratitude went up as the seven of the regulars stepped around the broken glass and headed to the game room.

"Okay," she agreed. "I'll stay at your house for the next couple of days, but only if you have plants. If I don't see so much as one green leaf then—"

"Boy Scout's honor," he promised with a hearty chuckle. "Promise."

Chapter Eighteen

Dropped off at the curb by the car service, Hawk slung his bag over his shoulder and headed up the gravel driveway. He stopped at his cast-iron double doors to punch in the key code. Their game against the Toronto Wolverines had been cancelled due to inclement weather, which meant he was home two days earlier than he'd originally planned.

The minute he heard about the break-in at Moe's, he'd panicked. Initially Hawk had no idea how to get Lexi to stay at his house, but he knew he wanted her to be safe. The whole plant idea had been quick thinking on his part.

He opened the door and stepped into his converted shipping warehouse. One of the dumbest ideas he'd ever had hadn't turned out that bad. Hawk dropped his bag in the entranceway and took in the large, indoor, towering Ficus trees he'd bought for immediate delivery minutes after Lexi had accepted his offer to stay with him.

A dreary film of gray seeped through the wall window that faced his garden. The natural colors from outside wove their way inside his house in a majestic manner. Several trees lined his entryway, providing a lively brightness that hadn't been there previously.

"Lexi?" His voice bounced around the concrete walls that suddenly felt cold. *Has it always been like that?* Hawk couldn't remember that large, empty feeling in the past. Mainly on the road, he didn't clock that much time in the place. He headed down the hall. Once he passed the living room, more gradients of blue and gray tones welcomed him. It was clinical in appearance, but he never considered the lack of warmth in his home. Serene maybe, but for the first time he realized this shit wasn't at all inviting.

"Trashcan999, you got the shot. Take it!" Lexi yelled. Picking up his pace, Hawk followed the sound of her sweet voice to his media room — the only spot in the whole house that he allowed a ridiculous display of his Y chromosome to shine. "Come on, you little fucking shit."

"Chill out, you bossy bag of bones!" The nasal twang of a teenage boy practically blew out his eardrums. Hawk turned the corner into the room and stumbled back a step. Lexi was instant eye porn. Surrounded by framed old jerseys, hockey sticks and awards, she sat half naked on the media room floor playing his Xbox.

As the game reflected back in her hot nerd glasses, he took in her teeny, tiny boy shorts and belly shirt. The pure lack of clothing was enough to make him hard, but with her smooth legs tucked underneath her body, the total recall of them around his waist came to mind.

Shit! Where Lexi was concerned, he was doomed. Up until this point, he'd behaved himself. However, he didn't think he could fake the nonchalant funk any longer. Contemplating his next move, he scratched his beard to hide his smile. *God, I'm into this woman.*

"Hey, you little tools, I've got to go." She vigorously tapped on the remote control.

"Why, grandma, is it time for your soaps?" Several of the little minions cackled in unison.

Hawk reluctantly tore his eyes away from her level ten cuteness that began at the top of the curly waves of her head down to her bubblegum-pink-painted toenails. Above his fireplace, where the big screen TV hung, Lexi's soldier avatar patrolled a busted village. On the side panel of the screen, it showed her teammates' icons and their whereabouts.

"Why do you guys want to do everything the hard way?" She sighed. She swiftly hit the controller, and a bomb exploded across every screen, except for hers.

"What the shit-stained-hell did you just do?" several teen baby voices hollered at the vision of lust in front of him.

"No one has that code. It's an urban legend. How did you get that code, Cutie32?"

Lexi stretched across the floor, reaching for the console, and she hit the power button, quickly muting all the obnoxious whining.

"Someone's home early?" Lexi made eye contact with him for the first time since he'd walked into the room.

"Game canceled." *Thank goodness!* He wouldn't have missed this for the world. "So…uh, glasses?"

She touched the round, black rims that covered her dainty face. "Yeah, I usually wear contacts, but—"

"Remy got it right," he muttered under his breath. She was definitely a hot nerd.

"Huh?"

"And the video game." Quickly changing the subject, Hawk hitched his thumb toward the system. He didn't get much use out of it. He had occasionally played from time to time, but in no way displayed Lexi's high level of skill.

"Oh, do you mind?"

"Of course not. I just didn't take you for a gamer."

When she held out her hand, Hawk reached out to help her stand up. *Goodie!* A better view of her body.

"Not a fanatic, but I dabble," she admitted.

"Confession..." His voice lowered to a register short of a growl.

"Can I hazard a guess?" Lexi stopped him. Already amused by her, Hawk nodded. "This" — she made the ta-da motion with her hands at her barely-there ensemble — "is some sort of eighties movie flashback. Am I right? I mean, those are the only movies you ever talk about, so-o..."

Damn, she'd hit that nail on the head. "Uh." He rubbed the corners of his mouth with his thumb and forefinger. "The movie *Tomboy* mixed with *Weird Science* is going on a loop in my head right now." He settled upon the truth. "Those two movies were cult classics."

"Gotta admit, I'm a little worried about this obsession of yours." As Lexi pushed her glasses back onto her face, her mouth turned down in a judgy pout.

"Those movies had great moral lessons."

"Most eighties movies objectified women's bodies. If the Me-Too movement could go back in time, they'd have a field day with that genre." Lexi placed her hands on her hips with a smirk.

"There may have been a boob or two on the screen, but the all-around wholesomeness of that decade suppressed those small moments of sexism," he admitted.

"Such as?"

While Hawk rocked back on the heels of his boots, he mentally accepted her challenge, despite his mind screaming, *It's a trap!* She was walking him straight into this fight with her distracting, sexy awesomeness.

"*Sixteen Candles*," he muttered.

"Final answer?" She raised her perfectly sculpted eyebrow in question.

"No, no, not that one." Sure, there was that cute table scene with the birthday cake, but the rest of that shit was sketchy. "Hold on. Let me think." Where was Alex Trebek from *Jeopardy!* when he needed him? Hawk wiped his brow, afraid that she would see she had him sweating.

"Here… I'll throw you one." Lexi took a step closer, leaving barely an inch of space between them. "It borders on stalkerish, but it's at least in the sweetest way possible…I mean, for the eighties."

"Honestly, that sounds like ninety-eight percent of the rom-coms back then."

"Puck," she called out, "play that song in the movie where the guy holds the boombox over his head."

Confused at what she was doing, he opened his mouth to say as much, but she put a finger to his lips to shh-h him. "*In Your Eyes* by Peter Gabriel, 1986." One of the most famous love ballads of the eighties blared over his sound system. Hawk could practically feel the surge of serotonin spark in his brain.

"How the hell—?"

"Sorry... I wanted to test a thing I was toying with, and since your place is perfect... Don't worry. It's not keeping a record of any conversations. The server is private and the app doesn't activate until five seconds after you call its name."

"Puck?" he asked.

"Easy enough to remember, I hope?"

Stunned speechless, he didn't answer her right way. The silent seconds that went by must have made her nervous, he assumed, by the way she bit down on that plump lower lip.

"I'll deprogram it before I go back to my place if it makes you uncomfortable."

"Uh, what was it you did before you came to Chicago?"

Tilting her head to the side, she ran her hand down her body. "Which movie does this outfit remind you of?"

He made a note to circle back to that question later, but his mind was overloaded with the soundtrack from *Say Anything* and every other eighties fantasy he could imagine. "Both. *Tomboy* was about a hot chick who could do anything a guy could do but better."

"And the other one?" Lexi placed her hand on the belt of his jeans.

Used to only the groupies pulling this aggressive sexy act, Hawk cleared his throat. He had stopped his whole snow cone runs in his twenties, which was the name they'd called the hockey groupies. They were great for one season, but once it was over, the taste for them was also gone. However, if he'd met Lexington Waters back then, he would have been seriously a goner. He swallowed back the urge to pounce. "*Weird*

Science, two nerds make the perfect woman to be their girlfriend."

"How is this moment anything like those movies?"

"Have you seen you?"

A low, meowing chuckle emanated from her.

Too tempted, he lowered his head to sniff her soft curls. Honeysuckle and pineapple filled his nose. Everything about Lexi meshed into this amazing hot nerd. "Okay."

"Hmm-m," he hummed.

"We have to exorcise this obsession out of you." In one swift motion she had his jeans unbuttoned and hand in his pants.

"Whoa." His hard dick jumped within her grip.

"This is the most eighties thing I can think of." She sank onto his custom jersey shaped rug, pulling his pants down with her.

"With the glasses on?"

"Of course." She practically swallowed his whole rod.

'*Oh, thank you,*' he mouthed as the woman he'd hard crushed on for months teased his dick. She slid her way up his pole, then pulled his tip out with a loud, smacking pop.

Lexi's porn star stare seemed to issue him a dare. Up for the challenge, he refused to glance away. While she tickled the head of his dick with her tongue, she pushed her glasses farther back onto her face. He groaned under the weight of her control, and pre-cum seeped out of his tip. She placed small kisses to the mushroom-head of his dick.

Not set up for this type of torture from this girl, Hawk slipped his rod into her mouth and gave it a few good pumps. He touched the back of her throat with his dick, and she choked on his length before he reached down and grabbed Lexi under her shoulders.

"Teasing over," he growled. Bringing her face-to-face with him, he took control of the situation and feverishly attacked her mouth.

Chapter Nineteen

Lexi had planned a whole day full of video games, merlot and pizza. If anyone had told her a fine-ass hockey player would come home early, she would have at least worn something sexy from Lady Fenty.

Instead, Hawk had walked in on her sporting nothing but her favorite bum-around clothes and cussing out the teen-turds. Needless to say, when he'd stepped into the room, she hadn't expected his reaction to her outfit.

Hot sex with an athlete wasn't on her list, but since one had shown up, why not? Lexi hadn't thought twice about dropping to her knees and controlling that dick. Sadly, he'd stopped her before she could really make him beg.

Snatching Lexi from her knees, he brought her nose-to-nose with him. Powerful and strong, Hawk bruised her lips with his before he maneuvered his tongue into her mouth.

"Hmm-m," she moaned. As she wrapped her arms around his neck, Hawk trailed his rough hand down the front of her stomach. His hazel eyes glowed while he slipped into her panties.

"Fu-uck your pussy," he huffed into her mouth. "So damn sexy." Lexi sucked on his tongue. For a split second, their eyes connected before he touched her clit. Thumbing her nub, he pumped his finger into her slick hole.

Gladiator strong, he held her with no effort and walked her toward his black leather couch. Turning around, Hawk plopped down on the cushion. Lexi gazed into the eyes of a man who was a beautiful blend of rock star and superhero.

As Hawk inched his way up the bottom of her tank, his big, hard hand gently touched her nipple. "So fucking soft," he muttered.

Lexi had never felt very feminine. With her bigger-than-life parents, she had no idea if it had to do with her techie background, her lack of girlfriends, or her shitty ex-husband. Josh had never made her feel sexy or pretty... Their relationship was more friends with benefits. In other words, she had a business partner who she occasionally screwed.

While Hawk softly caressed her breasts with his rough hands, Lexi realized everything about him was a contradiction. Hard on the outside, soft on the inside, he played one of the most brutal sports, but he was all heart. She honestly didn't know what to make of him.

Grabbing her tank from the bottom, she pulled it over her head, allowing him full access to her breasts. A million thoughts raced through her mind as he leaned forward and flicked her nipple with his tongue.

The one thing that frightened her the most was that if she wasn't careful, she would lose herself completely to this man—and she couldn't do that again.

Batting away the nagging swirl of emotions that distracted her from immense pleasure, she moved against his crotch. Her underwear created a thin barrier between them, which muted the sensation of skin-to-skin contact.

"Didn't I warn you about teasing me?" Hawk cupped the underside of her breast to lather her nipple into a pebbled bud.

"Oh," she moaned. Lexi wanted it all—slow, fast, and hard. While she was struggling to get her underwear off, he took her whole breast into his mouth. Hawk swirled his tongue around her nipple, causing her pussy to clench.

"Sssshit," she hissed, failing horribly at freeing herself from her underwear. In the least sexy manner possible, she kicked them off. Grabbing his hard rod, she lifted her ass up enough to split her pussy lips with his tip.

"*Argggh*." He dropped his head back on the arm of the couch with a groan as she slid down his shaft.

Rotating her hips, she moved up and down on his dick. A million sensations attacked her. Elation bloomed in her chest and warmed her entire freaking being.

Hawk placed his huge hands on her hips to control her movements. The last year had handed her a storm of crap. Lexi deserved this sexual high that would release her from obligation and duty, even if it was for a short amount of time.

As she allowed the strong smell of wood, sage, and citrus to consume her senses, Lexi rode the jock's dick.

Fuck! Hawthorne Maze was the whole package, but she refused to think about anything other than getting off.

When he closed his eyes and bit his lips, a wistful expression softened the athlete's face. She leaned forward to kiss his perfect mouth. Lexi worked her thigh muscles and slid up and down, up and down.

Tightening her pussy walls around his shaft, she hit her natural high with a scream. Hawk's breath quickened, and Lexi fell on top of him in a lump. Seconds later, he followed her to the other side of bliss.

She didn't know how long they had lain quietly on the couch entangled within each other's arms before the doorbell rang.

"Lexi."

"Huh?"

"The door?"

"Oh yeah." She lifted her head up to peer into the hazy blur of his eyes. "Pizza." Her chin bounced off his hard chest from the rumble of his chuckle.

"He's right on time." Hawk planted a kiss on her forehead and rolled her to the side to grab his pants. While she studied the awesome view of him shoving his hard ass into denim, he hopped his way out of the room.

Flipping on her back with a groan, Lexi attempted to stifle the spinning thoughts that battered around in her orgasm-addled brain. If she weren't careful, she would fall for a that freaking man.

Chapter Twenty

A half-hour before game time, the Northern Royals stretched out their muscles in the gym. Still early in the season, the press deemed the team's performance off to a shaky start. No one had taken into account the number of players who had retired or got traded. Sports analysts had made it seem as if they were entitled babies who should have been able to instantly gel together.

In less than an hour, they would play against one of their fiercest competitors and would need to be on their A game to pull it off. Less worried about stomping the Texas Wigeon into oblivion, Hawk was more concerned about Lexi rooting him on from the stands. He rarely invited anyone other than Knox, and that douche had been too busy this last year to even notice the freaking season had begun.

"Yo, man, you coming?" Marco called from the door.

Hawk did ten more reps and huffed out a breath. On the last count, he finally noticed the place had emptied out. Next were ice warmups.

"I forgot to ask how you were doing since they pulled that little stunt on your drink."

"Huh?" He snatched his towel off his bag, then wiped the sweat from his forehead.

"Yeah, I heard from Tina." Hawk screwed up his face in question. "The brown-haired Jugs girl." He cupped his hands in front of his chest. "Anyway, she told me one of the rooks had this bright idea to lace your drink with some muscle-enhancing supplement. It was supposed to give you the runs, but they didn't know you had diabetes."

"Are you shitting me?"

Marco held up his hands in a 'don't shoot the messenger' stance. "We're not talking geniuses, dude. These idiots barely made it out of high school."

"Those little fucks could have killed me."

"Yeah, well, do you want to get them back...reverse pinch?"

"Seriously?"

"Why not?" Marco shrugged. "Someone has to teach them a lesson."

The play called for two guys to crowd the opposition from both sides, which would allow one of them to steal the puck. Northern Royals' offense worked hard on getting their toddlers out of these types of jams. However, since his teammates were narcissistic assholes, Hawk was up for the challenge.

"If the opportunity presents itself, I'm in."

"Cool." Marco threw him a lazy salute before he opened the door to the locker room. Hawk grabbed his water bottle off the floor and squirted a good amount in his mouth.

Nothing in his life seemed to make much sense, but he'd never seen this type of shit coming. In the past he would have stormed into the locker room and beat every single one of those degenerates into a bloody mess. Instead, Hawk reached down and grabbed his bag with a sigh. *This adulting crap sucks.*

* * * *

Lights flashed around the rink after their fifth goal of the night. The Northern Royals were tied in the third quarter. If it went into overtime, they would be forced into a shootout, which meant whoever scored first won. Chords from Nu Shooz *I Can't Wait* filled the stadium.

Hawk glided across the ice, scanning the bleachers to catch a glimpse of the angel in pink. Lexi waved at him from her seat. The beauty stood out from the crowd. Of course, Andre would say it was due to her being the only black person in the whole arena, but Hawk knew better.

Lexi was freaking effervescent.

Until this moment he didn't even know what that word meant, but the moment he saw her practically glowing in a sea of blue and black jersey-dressed fans everything had become very clear to him.

With less than three minutes left in the play, he kept a good pace with the forward as two guys from the opposing team boxed in Axel. Marco nodded at him from across the ice. Once the forward slid the puck to him, he could then knock it closer to their goal.

Instead, Axel hit the puck to Marco, who in turn passed it to Hawk. He pivoted around the Texas

Wigeon's forward, who was hot on his trail, and skated his ass toward their net to sink the puck into their goal. While the crowd went wild, he sailed by Axel and threw a cool wink in the young'uns' direction.

* * * *

No one had told Lexi about the unbalanced nature of Black Fridays. First came Thanksgiving, where American families consumed a ton of huge, flightless birds. The meal within itself was enough to trick a human body into a deep lethargic coma until the following Monday. However, millions of people who had scarfed down the equivalent of two Ambiens still found enough time to go shopping—and for *hours,* no less.

After working double shifts for three days straight, Lexi stumbled around Hawk's house in a blur. "Puck, make coffee." *Did I put a mug under the machine's dispenser?* If not, she would find a mess in the kitchen.

With her eyes half open, Lexi staggered from the bed and felt her way to the bathroom. This was her last day before she could finally take off. Stepping into Hawk's massive bath cave, she flipped the water lever to the far right. The sprays hit her from all angles, and Lexi sunk into the massaging beat from the showerheads.

"*Argh,*" she moaned. Lowering her head, she allowed the water pulse to attack her knotted muscles.

"Now you know why I had a multi-sprayer installed." Hawk's gruff voice was slightly more comforting than the pulse from the showerhead.

Beads of water slipped down her face. Lexi opened her eyes to peer at him underneath her wet lashes. He'd played two away games with one day off in between, and Lexi didn't know how he had the energy to even stand up.

"How don't you live in here?" she asked.

"Trust me. It's hard." Fully dressed, he stepped into the shower. Water from all angles drenched his shoulder-length hair. As Lexi wiped the droplets out of her face, he closed in the space between them, sweetly brushing her lips with a kiss. Pressing her bare chest against his soaked T-shirt, she clung to a solid wall of muscle.

"Going to the bar?" he murmured.

In Lexi's hard-fought rise into the tech world, she had never been this bone-weary. At the beginning of her career, she'd pulled all-nighters that hurt way less than twelve hours on her feet in a blues bar. Laying her head against his chest, she inhaled his woodsy, spicy scent that had a touch of vanilla and smoky ember.

How the hell does this man always smell so freaking good?

"Simone's kid got sick again, but this time shared the germy icks with her."

"Tough break," he murmured into her wet hair. After her shower, she would have to work gel into her waves to keep them tame, since she didn't have the energy to do much more than that.

"Let me get cleaned up first." He leaned down and pecked the tip of her nose with his lips. "Then I'll join you at the bar."

"Mmm-hmm, that sounds good," she admitted.

He traveled his hand slowly over her breast, past her stomach, straight down to her pussy. Hawk strummed the small tuft of pubes right above her clit.

"Got a minute?" he asked, inching his way down to her pussy lips.

"Just one?" she responded.

Hawk tapped her nub with his index finger — a methodic rhythm that forced her to arch into his touch.

"Maybe two… Give me a least two?" He slipped his middle finger into her pussy.

"Ahh-h," she sighed. Leaning against his chest, Lexi hiked her foot against the wall. "For you, Maze, I'll allow you a good six."

"I promise I'll do the utmost to make the best of it." He sucked her bottom lip in his mouth and pulled his finger in and out of her wet pussy.

"Come for me, baby." Inside of her wet hole, Hawk increased his speed, while he lowered his head to suck on her nipple.

"Hmm-m."

Lexi rocked her hips to the silent beat he made as he held her leg up and used his finger to fuck her. Hopefully, this was his first go of it, before he would use his awesome dick on her.

Pretty sure she would be late for work, she tangled her tongue with his. Screaming into his mouth, Lexi was positive she could come even harder with the next orgasm.

"Okay," she moaned. "Seven minutes." Hawk chuckled in her ear as he unleashed his rod from his pants to push into her wet and willing body.

Chapter Twenty-One

Wall-to-wall bodies covered every free inch of Moe's. Black Friday was no joke. Hawk hadn't had a single moment to talk to Lexi since he'd stepped into the bar. In the span of two weeks, he'd played four away games and had every intention of sleeping off his muscle aches.

"Three beers on tap, two strawberry daiquiris and a gimlet," the waitress barked at him.

Moe's was in the weeds, and after he'd witnessed Lexi's sleep shower, he didn't have the heart to leave her short a bartender.

From time to time, he sneaked a few glances in her direction. She flitted around resembling a very sexy Betty Boop, Toni Braxton, smattered with Dorothy Dandridge fembot.

Around three p.m., the rush finally slowed down long enough for him to take his break in the alley. A niggling thought had messed with his head ever since their date in California. Over fifteen minutes he'd searched the web for her previous job. Something in tech, he recalled. Once he'd found her, then maybe he'd spot a picture of the dude who had grabbed her arm in California. However, he'd come up empty. There was no trace of Lexington Waters anywhere.

Hawk didn't usually check on the women he dated. Generally, they weren't around for any length of time or simply couldn't hold his attention longer than the start of next season. Lexi, on the other hand, had quickly turned into a different story, and he wasn't entirely sure how he felt about it.

Why is this bugging me? Maybe it had been the familiarity. Unable to place the guy's face without a proper name, his web search had been rendered useless.

Grabbing the handle, he opened the back door and went back into the bar. Dodging the harried servers who ran in and out of the kitchen, he shoved the swinging door to the bar. The foot traffic had picked back up tenfold, and the main floor was crammed with people.

"Hey," he snagged the woman of his filthy dreams by her waist before she could pass him, "the team has this event."

"Do tell?" Lexi smiled up at him as if she were interested, instead of shoving him off and bitching for messing with her time. Feeling put on the spot, he cleared his throat and resisted the urge to duck his head in embarrassment.

"The team has a convention deal around Christmas, and—"

Lexi's delicate face twisted into a judgy frown. Since they hadn't labeled their relationship yet, Hawk suddenly felt the need to tread lightly. "The team does a couple of stops, then we have the rest of the week to chill."

"Ooookay."

"Wow, you're not going to make this easy on me, are you?" He chuckled.

The corners of her lips curled at the ends, blooming into a big, sweet smile. "No," she said, shaking her head slowly, "I'm not."

"Lexi, would you like to spend Christmas with me?"

"Sure, sounds fun." She slapped him on the chest with the back of her hand. "That wasn't too hard, now was it?" Turning away from him with a wink, she headed into the kitchen while he walked back to the bar.

Hawk would have skipped on his way, but he'd made enough of a fool himself. One of the high tables had totally ear-hustled their whole conversation — the little, gray-haired ladies' thumbs-up was a big tip off.

Apparently, people craved liquor and blues music during the holidays more than any other time in the year. Thrown back into the rush, he made a ridiculous amount of frou-frou drinks. Lost in the performer's raspy voice, he quickly poured five crafts in a row. The teen's mournful melody filled the bar.

"My wife said that vein in your head was bulging, but damn." Knox shoved his way to the bar and put out his hand. Hawk hadn't seen him in weeks, so he fist-bumped his friend and went back to slinging the booze. "Thinking hard, big guy."

"Remy's not here."

"If she wasn't, how would I know you asked Lexi to the National Hockey Convention?"

Hawk threw the bar rag over his shoulder and sighed.

"Do not give me shit about this." Hawk reached down to grab three bottles from the refrigerator under the bar.

"Man, I think it's great—"

"But?" Hawk uncorked the bottles, then slid two of them across the bar to the college girl waiting. The last one he set in front of Knox.

"A marketing event is not the best time to spring the hockey wives on her. I mean, you want to keep her around, right?"

"They're not that bad."

"From what I've heard, they are." Knox took a hearty swig of his beer. "Now where the hell is my wife?" he asked once he'd swallowed.

"Not here, I would have seen her."

Lexi had picked that perfect moment to slide into the bar area and nudge him with her elbow. She pointed to a high table in the far corner.

"Ah crap, sorry," Hawk apologized. A group of dudes surrounded her. Usually he shooed the brave fools, who tested out their courage, away. "I'll get rid of them."

Knox grabbed his arm. "That's a new haircut."

He took another glimpse at the table. Remy had whacked a few inches off her hair. It framed her face and fell to the nape of her neck.

"Ooookay." Hawk shook his head. He couldn't begin to figure out what the hell was going on with these two. Usually his best friend wanted to fight any guy who looked at Remy cross-eyed.

"That's how she wore it college," he murmured in a dreamy tone. A fluffy cardigan hid her baby bump. No wonder why the besotted idiots were hypnotized by Knox's hot wife.

"Good to know. Do you want me to get those morons away from her or nah?"

"Are you crazy?" he squeaked.

"Huh?" Hawk stopped to stare at him, confused by the sudden appearance of red welts that rushed up Knox's neck.

"He's right." Lexi slapped him on the back, then pointed. "You're going to want to see this."

As cheap-suit guy leaned toward her with every one of his thirty-two teeth on display, Remy pulled her sweater away. The reaction was instant recoil from the sight of her five-months-preggo stomach. All the regulars laughed at the man's discomfort.

"Can you do me a favor and watch the kids tonight?" Knox asked in a rush.

"What the hell, man?" Hawk threw the towel onto the bar with a groan. He was completely ready to call it a night. "I just did a triple. You know that." Beyond tired, he could barely keep his eyes open.

Turning away from Hawk, Knox faced Lexi. "What do you say...two sweet baby girls, some wine and a lakeview scene."

"If it's so great, why don't you just stay home?" Lexi asked.

"Well, I uh..."

"Tell her," Hawk urged.

"Do I have to say it?" Knox pouted, which was completely pathetic for a grown-ass man with his sports pedigree.

"Yes," they said in unison.

"There's no way in hell I'm getting laid if we stay home."

"Because?" Hawk pushed, mildly amused at Knox's dilemma.

"Don't do this, man." He hung his head low and shook it.

"Because—"

"They're spoiled—and it's my fault," Knox confessed. "Rotten to the point they would drive Nanny McPhee straight to the insane asylum. Only Hawk or Dahl can watch them without my neighbors calling DCFS, SWAT and the National Guard simultaneously."

"Seriously?" Lexi chuckled. "When you put it like that…the answer's no."

Hawk laughed hard for the very first time in days, and it felt light…fucking great in fact. A gut-buster at the expense of Knox was the best medicine.

"Fine." Hawk petered off. "I'll call Moe to close, and we'll head over there in an hour."

"Whoa." He swiped his hand across his brow. "I thought I'd have to beg. Thanks, bro." Knox practically pushed his way to the front door. "Tell my lady I'm waiting in the car."

"Crazy nut…" Leaning away from the thick crowd, he turned his big body to face her. "I'll watch the kids if you want to go home and get some sleep."

"And experience the worst case of FOMO? No thank you," Lexi told him. "In for a penny, in for a pound."

Chapter Twenty-Two

Dressed head to toe in tutus and tiaras, they sat on the floor in front of the kiddie table. Hawk cradled Sadie, Knox's youngest daughter, in his arms, while Lexi held Nyla in her lap. Apparently the three-year-old had a battery charger hooked in her back. She had zoomed from one place to the next the moment they had arrived.

Thankfully, her dad had been available. An hour before the last performer had taken the stage, Moe had strutted into the bar. Since he would be jamming out with his old crew until closing time, they had felt comfortable enough to take off for their babysitting shift.

From the moment they'd stepped foot into the most beautiful lakefront home she'd ever seen, two little terrors had taken them hostage. No doubt, the cutest ones she had ever laid eyes on, but tiny terrors, nevertheless.

"After this, we'll color your feet, Uncle Hawk." The toddler stretched her munchkin body across the kiddie table.

As the little girl chattered endlessly, she painted Hawk's fingernails the most obnoxious rainbow colors imaginable.

"We probably should have started with my feet," he grumbled. Sloppy to a comedic level, Nyla moved over to his left hand.

"No, because last time we never made it to your hands, and…" Lexi peeked over, and to her surprise, the kid had fallen asleep mid-manicure.

"Wow, that was fast."

"Yep. She kept those eyes open longer than usual." He drew his hand from underneath the sleeping baby and stood up with more grace than she could have mustered. "Don't move."

Hawk worked his way around to her side of the table and gently retrieved Nyla off her lap. After crossing the room with both kids in his arms, he laid them down in a pink princess tent.

"Not your first time doing that, I take it." Lexi smirked. He came back to her and held out his hand. She placed her palm into his, and with no effort he pulled her out of the toddler chair.

"At the orphanage, all the older kids had to help with the babies, so I'm actually better at this than Knox." He guided her to the playroom door, flipping off the overhead light. Before they slipped out of the room, a pretty glow of stars and hearts circled around the ceiling. Lexi heavily considered quitting the bar to become Remy and Knox's nanny. Hanging out with kids all day seemed a hell of a lot better than dealing with drunks and the all-around mess that had become her life.

"Have you ever looked for your biological parents?" she asked. Hawk held her hand while they headed down the hallway that opened to the living room. The view out of the panoramic window took her breath away. Every part of the house felt regal and spacious.

"No." While Hawk walked to the kitchen, Lexi gravitated toward the lake view. "I didn't want to know anyone who would give up a kid like that, but the older I get, the more curious I've become." Lexi glanced over her shoulder at Hawk, who pulled down two glasses from the cabinet. "Maybe after I retire," he said, opening the refrigerator, taking out the pitcher of iced tea and pouring a glass. "I'd have more time on my hands, I guess." Hawk put away the pitcher and grabbed an open bottle of wine. The effortless way he moved in the kitchen, told Lexi that Hawk obviously knew his way around Knox's house.

She faced the window again. There wasn't a star in sight, but the lake waves hadn't frozen near the shore. The view was amazing. Unfortunately, she was dead tired, and it had felt like a million years since this morning. Lexi wished she were more awake to enjoy the place.

"The older I get, the more I want to know why," he said. Soft in his steps, Hawk held out a glass.

Regardless of her current exhausted state, Lexi welcomed her time with Hawk and the kids, and she accepted the wine. It helped take her mind off all this SugarTech mess.

"They could be looking for you," she offered.

"Doubt it."

Lexi slid her glance from the calm lake view over to the big man. Hawk seemed to unconsciously clench and unclench his jaw. During his hockey game, she'd spotted his tell. *Did I hit a sore spot?*

Putting his arm around her shoulder, he pulled her into his side. "Life doesn't generally work like that, at least not for me," he admitted, placing a kiss onto her forehead.

* * * *

The Knoxes' night view didn't hold a candle to the morning sunlight that poured into the house. Lexi had barely slept. Josh had sent her another video, this time from a different angle. He'd even managed to bypass her phone's home screen. If she'd left her phone unattended, anyone at the bar could have seen it.

While the bacon sizzled in the pan, she flipped the pancakes on the hot plate and considered giving up her shares of SugarTech. She didn't want to live her life in constant fear, always expecting the other shoe to drop.

"What is that smell? Is that home cooking in *my* house?" Remy stepped into the kitchen. Lexi caught the cat who ate the canary smile that spread across her hot-girl face.

"Walk of shame looks good on you."

Remy shoved her hair back and did a little twirl. "It's been forever. Thanks."

"Is that bacon?" Knox stepped into the kitchen, bedraggled and sexy as ever. He grabbed his wife by the waist. "Who knew the stove worked?"

"That's all I'm saying," Remy replied.

Lexi turned her attention back to the food with a chuckle. She needed something to keep her mind busy, and cooking was the only thing she could think to do. Lexi transferred the bacon to a platter, then poured the eggs into the frying pan.

"Is the big oaf still asleep?" Knox asked.

"Yes, and in his own room, no less," Lexi pointed out, amazed at the closeness of the childhood friends.

"Hawk is here so much he might as well live here." Knox tossed his jacket over his shoulder. "Besides, he's always been a hard sleeper. I'm going to go slap his ass into the waking world, but first I'll check on the girls." He bent down to peck his wife's cheek before he walked toward the playroom.

"Are you staying with Hawk for the weekend or the whole convention?"

"Ah, I think the week." Lexi sprinkled seasoning on the eggs, then the cheese.

"Word of advice?" Remy offered.

"I'll take it any way that I can get it." She grabbed the pan's handle and scraped the eggs onto the platter with the bacon.

"Sports wives are tough. If it gets hard, promise you'll call me."

After flipping off all the burners, she turned to face Remy. "I'm sure I've dealt with worse."

"Trust me." The pretty woman reached for a grape out of the fruit bowl and popped it into her mouth. "This will be a brand-new experience for you."

"That bad?"

"Take it from someone who came into the wife game late… Watch your back."

"Come on." Lexi tugged at the sleeves of Hawk's sweatshirt. The cotton number fell to her knees, but she kept it cute by wearing her black leggings. "These women couldn't possibly be that bad."

"Have you ever seen any of the *Real Housewives*…I mean New York, Beverly Hills, Texas even?"

Lexi shrugged in reply, she honestly couldn't remember. "Maybe once or twice."

"Times all that bat-shit crazy by ten and boom, you've got the hockey wives. The only group that can top them is the baseball wives—and that's for totally different reasons."

A moment of panic rolled through her stomach, causing a flood of spit to coat her mouth. Lexi used the back of her sleeve to wipe her lips. On top of everything going on in her life, she didn't need another complication. "But we're just...you know."

"No"—Remy shook her head with a crazy 'I smelled poo' frown—"I don't know."

She lowered her voice to a whisper. "We're just fuck buddies."

As Remy made her way around the kitchen island, she snorted. "Yeah." She grabbed a plate from the pile Lexi had set out. "Hawk doesn't bring fuck buddies to watch my kids. Sorry, sweetie. You two have something, whether you've labeled it or not."

If Lexi added everything together—the bar, SugarTech and Josh—there was no room for a relationship with a hot-ass hockey star on her plate.

"Technically, Knox asked me to babysit."

"Of course he did. How else would he have gotten Hawk to come? Mmmhmm-m." Remy groaned. "This bacon is delicious, and I don't even eat meat... Must be the alien gestation happening inside of me."

"Baby, right? You meant baby?" Lexi nodded at Remy's growing belly.

"Potatoes, pa-ta-toes. Oh shit! Are those hash browns?" she squealed once she saw the golden-brown shreds on the counter behind the bottle of maple syrup.

While one of the most gorgeous momma-bears mauled her Top Chef breakfast presentation, Lexi seriously reconsidered her poor life decisions.

Chapter Twenty-Three

Everything in Aspen was blinding white displayed with twinkling lights. From the top of the mountains that lorded over the city, down to the slick streets, there wasn't a speck of color. If Lexi had thought Chicago winters were bad, nothing had prepared her for Aspen.

Santa Claus had shit snow onto the entire town. Aspen, Colorado's winter season was on a whole other freaking level. Lexi had taken the week off to spend with Hawk.

With no expectation for the wives'-girlfriends' itinerary past shopping, she'd immediately been thrown into a meet and greet. Different marketing franchises had taken over the pretty city, pitching their products to the professional players. Fans crushed the resort town during market week to get a picture with the teams—or even catch the latest technology revolving around their favorite sport.

Hawk had explained all this to Lexi before she'd left the bar in the capable hands of Simone and her father.

Since Moe had been feeling better, he'd been happy to babysit the bar for her.

Dressed in a form-fitting, ribbed, cream turtleneck dress, she stuck out worse than a sore thumb amongst the 1950s-styled wives. Lexi strolled into the girly tearoom of the ritzy boutique house and instantly felt out of place. Instead of requesting sexy winter gear, everyone was expected to dress for high tea, huh?

"Ladies!" A statuesque platinum blonde clapped her hands. "We have an itinerary to stick to. If you would please follow me to the China Room and sit with your team wives."

What the hell is a 'team wife'?

As Lexi darted her gaze around the room for the Northern Royals table, a quiver of nerves twisted her gut. Remy had warned her to skip this part, but she figured what would be the harm. Perhaps she could learn something about hockey, since she wasn't exactly an expert on the subject.

"Sorry, hon. This table is for the Royals… You might want the Florida table." The woman mostly made up of variant shades of blonde, yellow, platinum and one or two strawberries all laughed in unison. Not getting the joke, she did a quick scan of the tearoom to find she was the only black woman there. *Probably in the whole damn city.*

Lexi bared her teeth in an awkward smile, hoping it would help her fend off these psychotic mannequins. While she was preparing to slowly back out of the event, a cute brunette grabbed her arm.

"Lexi, right? This is Hawk's girlfriend," she announced to the table.

Friend, she almost corrected her, but realized she not only lived with Hawthorne Maze, she also dicked the sexy man down on a regular basis.

"I'm Tanya and this is…" Everyone's name went by in a blur since they appeared to be octuplets of some sort.

After she took her seat, she found herself heavily zoning out. The main Stepford wife spoke at length about the hockey wives' roles including marketing and how they could help their hockey player-mate with long-term career moves.

"Boring as fuck, right?" Tanya leaned over and whispered in her ear about a half hour into the worst tea party ever. Lexi snickered. She honestly couldn't wait for this to be over.

Twenty minutes later, the ridiculously boring luncheon had finally ended. The ladies mingled around the tearoom, chatting it up with one another. Lexi found herself at the bar in the swanky little boutique downing a martini.

She checked her phone, hoping she could meet Hawk back at the cabin to rub one out. *When the hell did I become this horny? Has my libido always been like this or does Hawk play a part?* Damn, Hawthorne Maze had definitely gotten under her skin. In the past she couldn't remember pulling her head out of her techie hole long enough to care about this stuff, but then again, a sexy-ass hockey player hadn't been factored into the equation.

"It's usually not that bad." Tanya popped onto the stool next to her.

"Are you kidding? 101 Marketing for Wives was adorable."

"And what is it that you do, not a wife?" Brandi, unnatural blonde number one, asked with a smirk. "Bartender, right?"

The dig at her wifeless status didn't bother her. However, she did wish she'd never been married to shithead Josh in the first place. "Yes, ma'am, I provide a supply to a demand."

"A booze slinger. Cute," Jessie or Jelly chimed in. Oh hell, blonde number two. Who was Lexi fooling? Tanya was the only one she would remember after this event.

"There's nothing wrong with serving drinks." The main speaker joined them. "She can take away from our tutorial and apply the same logic to her job."

"Except" — Lexi sipped her drink, savoring the little bit of alcohol she had left. Clasping the stem of her glass in her hand, she resisted the urge to get shitfaced on such a wonderfully colorless day — "instead of waiting for your agents to bring their clients sponsors, or continually using the same ones," Lexi said, "for example like Nike or Gatorade, who saturate the market, the wives can create an app featuring the leading companies in the stock market and startups. Go through these businesses and create a *marriage* of sorts" — she used her hands and interlocked them for visual effect — or she was more drunk than she thought — "where the wives could provide a need with their player spouses. Also, you can work in a charity aspect with the partnership and include into the deal whatever your agent hammers out. In other words, it's a fast and easy way to make a buck while merging a charitable aspect to the players, which is the type of sponsorship that is a good look for everyone all around."

As her phone went off in her left hand, Lexi chugged the rest of her drink. Since she didn't recognize the ring tone, she didn't bother to check. Instead, she scanned the faces of all the women who had joined her at the bar. "Yeah." She nodded her head at them, not entirely sure if what she'd said had sunk into their super-tanned heads or not.

"This is a joke, right?" Brandi scoffed. "I mean, showing a bit of tit and selling booze doesn't exactly mesh with the type of work we're doing here."

"Ah, actually" — the guest speaker held up her finger — "it's a solid idea. Would you mind if I talked to you about it more later?"

"Sure," Lexi told her. "But first I need to" — *get laid*, she omitted — "grab a nap. I have jet lag. The high altitude here is doing a number on me." She set her glass on to the bar. "Nice meeting you guys. It has been a pleasure." Hoping the sarcasm came across clearly enough, she headed for the coat rack and out of the dainty boutique shop.

Chapter Twenty-Four

The early part of Hawk's day had been spent shaking hands with team sponsors and fans. He opened the door to the three-level stunner made up of wood and warm earth tones. With a bit of time between events, he wanted to see Lexi... Correction, he needed to lay eyes on her.

"Lexington Waters, where's your pretty little ass?" he yelled, stepping into the cabin. Usually he breezed through these functions without much socializing. Unfortunately, the Northern Royal's management wanted him to participate with team activities all week long. That's why he'd rented this cabin and the two next door for the gang. His team was one thing, but the people he considered family were something else entirely. Knox, Andre and their crew would join them later in the week.

"Lex?" While Hawk jogged up the winding wooden staircase, he loosened his tie. "Hey." She slipped around the loft area into the main bedroom and saw that the remains of the sun brightened the bedroom from the west. Brilliant gradients of red, burnt orange and hazy purple flooded into the open door from the balcony.

"Amazing, huh?" Lexi poked her head out of the closet, wearing nothing more than a meager slip that barely covered her athletic body. Her small breasts, tiny but perky, caught his eye.

"Depends… Are we talking about the sun or you?"

"Ah, tell me more." She disappeared into the closet with Hawk close on her heels.

"Totally and completely truthful." Short on time, Hawk didn't want to waste this small window convincing Lexi with words. Flipping off his suit jacket, he tossed it on the granite island.

"How was your meet and greet?" she cooed. Ducking her head low, she threw a saucy smirk over her shoulder.

"Lame as fuck," he nearly panted. Hawk could hardly wait to be inside her. "And what about your meeting?" he asked. Super horny, he still wanted to appear thoughtful.

Lexi provided him with a healthy chuckle. "Probably lamer."

He unbuttoned the sleeves of his shirt and rolled them up his arms.

"Now don't tell me you came here thinking you were going to get—"

"What?" he pushed, attacking the first four buttons on his shirt with every intention of getting messy. He hoped she would say filthy things to him.

"Laid, pussy—or just your general 'some'. Did you think any of those things were going to happen?" She plopped her little fist on her hip.

Hawk rubbed his hand against his medium-sized beard. A superstition among players, they let their hair grow out during the season. By the time spring rolled around, he would be a full-blown mountain man. He honestly couldn't wait to get the thick shit off his face.

"Actually" — he closed in the gap between them, gently tilting her chin up with his index finger — "I was hoping for all three." Pecking her pouty lips, he eased his tongue into her mouth and tasted the tingly sting of alcohol.

Fuck, he couldn't get enough of her. That's why he'd rushed back to the cabin when he had little-to-no time between events. Lexi was more intoxicating than any drug, and he needed a good dose to keep his blood flowing. She tilted her head to the side, allowing him to drag his lips across her lovely neck before he sucked on her smooth skin.

"Turn around, baby," Hawk murmured, licking the spot on her neck that pulsed with her heartbeat. Obliging his request, Lexi faced the island, planting her hand on the granite top. Since he didn't have long, he tickled his fingers north to pull her slip over her pert bubble ass. "No undies?"

"Easy access."

"Dammit, Lexi, I believe you're the most considerate person I've ever met."

"Show me how much you appreciate it…"

"Gladly." Hawk sank to his knees and squeezed her ass. Starving, he ran his hand over her plump pussy lips. Lexi hummed low as he reached up and slapped her cheek.

"Oh," she cooed.

Dipping his head low, he dove between her pussy lips to feast. Hawk sucked her lips into his mouth.

"Mmmhh," he groaned at the salty sweet taste of her. Hawk tilted his head up and dragged his tongue through her core. Reaching up, he flatted her back with the palm of her hand, forcing her to raise that beautiful ass even higher.

Accepting the delicious treat she presented to him, Hawk spread her pussy lips with his fingers and leisurely licked her nub. Back and forth he spanked her clit with the tip of his tongue before he went all in to devour her wet pussy.

Lexi bounced her little ass gently on his mouth as her breathing quickened. Sucking hard on her clit, Hawk suctioned his lips onto her pussy to tickle, nip and tease her channel.

"Oh wooow!" she screamed, while going limp on top of the closet island. Wasting no time, he stood up while he fumbled with his pants. The need to be inside Lexi overrode every one of his senses. Splayed for him like in a pornographic picture, Lexington Waters checked every erotic box on his list. He wanted to feel her body wrapped around his cock ASAP.

Hawk licked her wetness from the edges of his lips and gripped his thick rod in his hand. Tapping his tip against her lovely ass, his pre-cum dribbled onto her brown cheeks.

Positive at any moment he would embarrass the shit out of himself and come too quick, he plunged into her wet folds.

"Sooo damn good, baby." He moaned. Hawk grabbed the back of her neck to plow her pussy. While he rode her from behind, he reached underneath her slim body to cup her perfect-sized breast and drive into her hard.

"Fufufufuuuck!" Lexi shouted.

Warm tingles shot through his entire body. Hawk swiveled his hips and sped up his pumps. He didn't know what to call the strong hold she had over him. Lexi brought a range of emotions into his life — and the highs were never ending.

As he buried his whole shaft into her pussy, a tight tingle started in his balls, begging him to release his load. He wouldn't think about a life where he would rely on someone to the point where it hurt — love was off the table — but this whatever it was, he could get used to.

Fighting off the emotions that wanted to highjack his beautiful XXX orgasm, Hawk focused all his attention on the pleasure her taut body provided him. He thrusted and fucked her hard. Lexi's tight pussy wrung him dry.

A wicked dose of adrenaline forced a lightheaded swell in his head to overrun all his senses. Still semi hard inside of the woman who was slowly disintegrating his bachelor life into a pile of ash, he reconsidered his resistance to the girl most successful.

Chapter Twenty-Five

After Hawk had provided her with great drive-by dicking, Lexi felt she had the presence of mind to handle the wives. They were expected to arrive for a cozy evening cocktail at the cabin. Each girlfriend or wife was scheduled to take a turn throughout the week to host events. Somehow, she must have pulled the short straw, because she was up first.

Setting out a simple spread, Lexi arranged a cheese tray that she'd paired with wine. If they wanted a more filling meal, they could politely visit one of those swanky restaurants in town.

Since she didn't see the point of experiencing fashion death in the high-altitude snow, Lexi wore a black blouse, jeans and boots. The minute the last hockey wife sashayed her ass out of the house, every stitch of her clothing would be on the floor in two seconds flat.

Someone lightly tapped at the door. Before she could set the party platter down on the coffee table, Daenerys

Targaryen from *Game of Thrones* stuck her head into the cabin.

"Knock, knock," she called out, while simultaneously inviting herself into the room. "Oh, hi! We didn't want to be too early, you know?"

Sure, Lexi could have picked the obvious choice and went with that nutjob Cersei, but she had a feeling this blonde bitch was a 'sneak attack' kind of crazy.

"No, I don't know." Tilting her head to the side, she feigned cluelessness. More often than not, Lexi was one of the few women working with all men in the room, not to mention the only black one. At this point in her life, she held a Ph.D. in microaggressions. Instead of apologizing for her rudeness, Brandi strolled into the cabin with her designer gang hot on her heels.

"Oh cute," Brandi commented in the most patronizing manner possible as she wiggled a pointy, jeweled finger at her cheese tray.

"Did more wives arrive?" The crew of women seemed to grow by leaps and bounds.

"No, this is all of us." Brandi beamed. The strange display of friendliness automatically put Lexi on alert.

"Let me help you in the kitchen?" The sweet chick from earlier, Tanya, hustled up next to her and tugged on her arm.

"Come, come." Brandi patted the seat next to her. "We have lots to get into."

Tanya closed her big, brown eyes with an audible loud sigh. When she reopened them, they had turned soft and shiny. With her shoulders hunched, she walked over to the brown leather couch and took a seat next to the blonde.

"So, what is it that you do? Bartender, right?"

"Yep." Feeling a setup of the bitch variety was on the horizon, Lexi's guard went up.

"And what did you do before that?"

"A little bit of this, a little bit of that." She sat down on the oversized leather seat and grabbed the wine bottle off the table to pour a glass. "Anyone?"

As Tanya raised her hand, Brandi elbowed her in the side. Lexi ignored the exchange and passed over the glass. No one besides a select few made eye contact with her.

"We were just wondering…like modeling perhaps?"

A random snigger from one of the women forced Lexi to gnash her teeth together. "Nope." She poured another drink, fixed her expression, and popped back up with a smile. "Wine?"

"Sure," a redhead who hadn't been at the earlier meeting said. "I'll take a glass."

"Ahem." Brandi threw them a dazzling predatory leer.

Waiting for the gotcha moment that Brandi had apparently come for, Lexi handed over the glass of wine.

"Because this little gem" — Brandi tapped on her cell phone before standing up and turning the screen toward the group — "tells me sooo much."

An amazingly clear shot of her getting pounded from behind by a faceless Josh covered the screen. Lexi's throat instantly felt dry to the point of scratchy hellfire. She wanted to scream but couldn't breathe. The carnal grunts from her sex video filled the air.

Nervous chuckles at her expense joined the noises from the floor while the rest of the women turned away from Lexi's breasts bouncing freely on the screen.

"Did you really think," Brandi bubbled out through fits of laughter, "you actually fit in...with us?" Louder giggles came from her minions, which cut through Lexi's rage to focus her anger. "We don't care how long Hawk's been around or who gave that fucker the pity popular vote." The blonde circled the room, holding up her phone for everyone to witness her unsolicited humiliation.

Years ago, Lexi had created an app to share videos with the closest phone. Since she couldn't see any practical use for it, she'd scrapped the idea. Josh, on the other hand, had apparently figured out a great way to utilize her work. When her phone had rang earlier at the meeting, it must have been her ex sending the video from yet another angle.

Lexi honestly didn't know what to do. She was frozen.

"But I got news for you, honey. We don't need no trash showing up on our playground trying to sell that shit to our kids."

"Huh," the redhead said, while she reached for a grape off the cheese platter. "What are we even talking about here?"

"That this isn't basketball. We have a good God-given sport that people like her aren't going to mess up."

"Oh please..." The redhead chomped on the fruit. "Who cares."

"We care." Brandi threw her hand up with a dramatic Southern preacher flair. "Our reputation will not be tarnished by whatever this is, and that's why you will *not* come to anymore games, parties or marketing events—"

The front door swung open, and Lexi jumped from the bang when it hit the wall. Unsure of the dual emotions that coursed through her veins, Lexi cleared her throat. Catching her bottom lip between her teeth, she held off a heavy attack of laughter or a nervous breakdown.

"Oh, dear. It seems we've not arrived in the nick of time," Dahl cooed. Bogged down with a big pot, she headed into the cabin.

"What movie is that from?" Remy walked in behind her with an arm full of bags. "Anyone, anyone?" she asked the hockey wives.

"*Practical Magic*," the redhead answered.

"Ding, ding, ding," Dahl said.

"What the hell? Why's Hawk's hag club here?" Brandi nearly shrieked. "Did you take a wrong turn between Tarjay and the g-het-o." She drew the words out with a shitty French accent, probably expecting a laugh from her audience, yet no one made a single peep.

As a strong dose of awkward energy strangled the room, the sound of Josh figuratively and literally screwing her played on Brandi's phone. Shame gobbled up her anger. The mere thought that people she liked would see Josh's handiwork froze Lexi to her spot.

"Jesus, for a pregnant chick, you can move..." Lashonda tumbled into the cabin, out of breath. "Did you drop the hammer on these bitches? Because whoo, this thin-ass air has me dizzy. I need a nap." The sexy vamp kicked the door closed with her heel.

"We were just getting to that part."

"There's not a damn thing you or any one of these tag-alongs can do to me that would matter," Brandi snapped. "You're fucking football wives."

Remy slipped off her floor-length coat, then placed it on the arm of the nearest chair. "Stupos never like it easy," she said while shaking her head. "Okay, Brandi Svenson previously Stallworth, one of the many publications I work for decided in the name of female empowerment not to run with a piece on you. This story included video of you giving the second season runner-up on *The Bachelor* an okay rim job."

Gasps of shock and surprise went up in a huge firework bloom around the room.

"A half-assed one, if you ask me." Lashonda snorted.

"Oh, Brandi!" one of the idiots cried.

"Big damn deal. Whatever advertiser drops Sven we can easily replace" — she snapped her fingers — "like that."

"But you told everyone you were a virgin, Brandi."

The redhead snorted. "And you bought that shit?"

"That will be ten dollars, Rem." Lashonda dropped down hard in the window seat by the door. "I told you the little hypocrite would flip it."

"Dammit, I'm hungry so I'm going to cut to the point. Dahl here owns a football team." Remy gestured toward the kitchen, as the classic beauty poked her head out of the opening and waved.

"So what?"

"Dahl here also has every single number to the hockey owners, GMs and managers on her speed dial. Now who wants to get their husband traded to a career-killing team? A show of hands, please."

"Shit," someone hissed.

"Exactly," Remy sang. "Now please pass your unlocked phones over to Lexi, then promptly get the fuck out."

"Wait a minute. I won a prize from earlier," the ballsy redhead spoke up.

While Lexi made swift work making sure the video hadn't been forwarded from any of their phones, Lashonda opened the door.

"That's right. You win a bowl of gumbo from a three-star winning Michelin chef," Remy told the redhead, then pointed to Tanya, who had at least appeared remorseful throughout the whole ordeal. "And you will stay here to collect all their phones and give them back later."

"No way... You can't keep our phones!" A grumble of outrage shook the room.

"Don't worry. I'll make sure they give them all back," Tanya said with a slight quiver to her voice.

"All right, hockey hookers, you heard the pregnant monster." Lashonda hustled the woman out of the door. "Let's go, let's go, let's go!" She clapped her hands together.

Lexi glanced up to see them file out one by one before she got to work.

As she wiped the video off the devices, she checked their emails, trash and cloud storage. Only a couple of the women had forwarded the video to one another. Tears blurred her eyes while she erased her ex-husband's latest soul-destroying stunt.

* * * *

The luxury house next door was stationed a half-yard away from the one Hawk had rented. He'd wanted his crew close but not piled on top of one other. Knox had hit him up on his cell, explaining their change in plans.

Hawk banged the door with the side of his fist. "Pizza delivery!" Knox flung open the wood door with both crying kiddos attached to his hip and a crazy expression set on his square face. "What's up, man?" He chuckled.

"Laugh now, but when it's your turn..." Knox walked toward the winding staircase to pass a screaming Nyla off to Bane's niece, Alana.

"Hey, kiddo." Hawk held up his hand for a high-five, but the twenty-something-year-old rolled her eyes and struggled to contain the full-blown toddler meltdown within her arms.

Dead on his feet, Hawk loosened his tie and took in the recreational cabin he'd rented out for all the children. Cozier than the one he'd gotten for Lexi and himself, this one reeked of. kid friendly. Between the three sets of families, they couldn't do too much damage to the place. Since Knox's boss didn't allow deadbeats on his watch, everyone had to pitch in. Thankful for the help, he figured it would at least give the return of his deposit a fighting chance.

"Thought you had a game?" Hawk asked his best friend.

All day he'd been held up in team marketing meetings. Kids, charity events, and the fans — it was his favorite stuff to do off the ice. Hawk loved the game but hated the business.

"We do. That's why this little side trip is hella inconvenient," Bane Winston replied. He stepped out of the kitchen clasping three beers in his hand. While he passed Knox a bottle, Bane's younger niece trotted down the stairs to take the other crying baby from Knox. Holding up his hand to the teen, this time Hawk got a hard slap in the middle of his palm for his trouble.

"Thanks, Cady," Knox told her. The big boss held the second beer out to Hawk. Usually he didn't touch the stuff, but what could it hurt? The day had been brutal. He nodded his head as Bane tossed it to him. *How long has it been since I had a cold one?*

Twisting off the bottle's top, he sighed. *Was that sad? Shit, maybe I shouldn't have it if my reaction was that strung out.*

"Anybody going to tell me what's going on?" Waiting for an answer, Hawk chugged the beer and instantly grew warm inside.

"No clue. The wives packed everything in a frenzy, then *boom*, we're in Aspen." Dark circles settled deep under Knox's eyes. The man looked a freaking mess. Hiding his chuckle behind a cough, he didn't feel sorry for Knox in the least. The Mavericks football team were in the middle of a hellacious season and the famous former quarterback carried the brunt of the stress.

"Fuck you." Friends since they were kids, they could easily read each other's mind and they both laughed.

"If the husbands were outranked during a critical season" — Hawk shook his head — "then there's definitely something up."

"Yeah, well, we have enough sense not to ask," Bane confessed. "We wanted to make sure everyone got settled in before we headed out in the morning." Hawk knew better than to dig deeper, even though his curiosity was getting the best of him. The wives were harder to crack than the mob.

Instead of worrying about what had brought everyone to the mountains earlier than scheduled, he settled back in his seat and tipped the rim of the beer bottle to his lips. Whatever storm was brewing would take place, no matter what he did. All he could do to prepare was hunker down and wait it out.

Chapter Twenty-Six

The R&B melody of Al Green's *Let's Stay Together* cleansed the rest of the negative energy the hockey monsters had left behind. Lexi tapped her foot up and down at a frantic pace. Screaming on the inside, she fought that insane urge to break things and rail at the world around her.

As laughter intermingled with Al's soulful groove, Lexi tinkered with one of Frankenstein bride's phones. She attempted to back trace the app Josh had used but couldn't find anything that would prove helpful in a court of law.

"How much longer?" Remy whined.

"Here." Lexi lifted her eyes away from the phone to see Dahl toss her a biscuit before she returned her focus back on the screen.

"The alien in my belly is hungry." Remy stuffed the appetizer in her mouth.

"Can you even eat seafood?" Lashonda asked. "I thought—"

"Zu shudup," Remy mumbled over her mouthful of food. "Shud de fud up!"

"That was my ex-husband," Lexi admitted barely louder than a whisper. "The asshole wants me to give up my shares in the company, and he's willing to do anything to make that happen."

When she didn't hear anything other than the beginning bars from New Edition's *Can You Stand the Rain*, she glanced at the five women. Afraid of what they were thinking, she swept her eyes across their faces. However, she didn't get the sense of self-righteous judgment from any of them.

"Josh used an old app I created to share the video," Lexi continued, as she fiddled with the phone in the palm of her hand. "Whoever is closet to you at the time it's sent will be able to accept documents, music, games, etc."

"Cool," Dahl said. "A complete time saver."

"That was the plan, but it had too many kinks," she lied, as she caught a quick flash of displeasure shimmer across Remy's face. "Anyway, it was one of many projects that didn't make it."

Lexi had never felt this vulnerable in her entire life. However, she owed these women an explanation. If that video had gotten out, that would have been all the ammunition Josh would have needed.

"Hey, I'm Bronwyn." The redhead waved her hand. "My ex is a bona fide shithead, but that" — she pointed at the phone in her hand — "that was revenge porn. What the hell did he hope to accomplish with it?"

"A leak." She pinched the bridge of her nose between her fingers and took a deep breath. "Under the morals clause in my contract, it would force the board to kick me off."

"What company is this?" Bronwyn chuckled. "Fucking Apple?"

"SugarTech."

"Oh damn!"

"Gurl."

"Shit!" A resounding chorus of shock went around the room.

"Huh?" Lashonda flopped over the back of the couch with a magazine. "Makes sense."

Instead of offering her a slew of empty platitudes, the group went back to the easy conversation only good friends could pull off. Since a million questions swirled in her head, Lexi gave up her on the data trace and set the phone down.

Remy nudged her with her knee, breaking her out of her daze of memorizing the geometric swirly patterns on the area rug.

"How did you know I needed help?" she asked the hot mom who passed her a glass of wine. While she waited for an answer, Lexi dreamily stared at the red liquid inside of it.

"Tanya." Remy chucked her thumb over her shoulder. "We all go way back. Her big sister is a football wife."

"Yeah. And believe me when I say the hockey wives are way worse," Tanya piped up, snagging her glass of wine off the coffee table. She took the seat across from her. "The video showed up on my phone after the luncheon. Brandi must have gotten it around that time. She was damn near orgasmic with the thought of 'hazing' you." She made quote marks with her fingers.

"We tried to get here sooner," Remy shrugged, "but you know how evil whores have no patience."

Lexi took a sip of wine as the women laughed at the truth. *Evil waits for no one.* Tired of the fight for her company that no longer seemed worth it, Lexi swiped at a wayward tear that managed to escape from her eyes. She'd promised herself that she wouldn't cry, but Josh's body blows had finally taken a toll on her.

He had continually knocked her down. Every time she'd gotten up, a little piece of her had gotten lost somewhere in the cracks of the pavement. Whether she wanted to admit it or not, Josh was out to destroy her.

"It's not your job to save me." She took a huge gulp of wine and felt that getting shitfaced drunk was on tonight's menu.

"But we've gotten so good at it," Lashonda cooed. Lexi chuckled.

It was true. She'd come to rely on these women in such a short amount of time, and she honestly didn't know how to repay them.

"Don't worry, honey. If the calvary hadn't arrived in time, we would have stepped in," Bronwyn told her. "I'm a hockey wife on the Southern White Tails' team, and this one right here is my best friend." She tipped her head in Tanya's direction.

"Also, she's a WWE championship winner," Tanya added.

Lexi narrowed her eyes to slits. Already embarrassed enough for one day, she didn't want to come off like a complete idiot, but she had no idea what WWE stood for.

"Wrestling," Bronwyn explained. "I beat grown men and women's asses for a living."

"Sexy," Lexi said with appreciation. As everyone laughed, she reached for the bottle of wine. "Are we good on this one?"

"Yeah, we can open another," Dahl called from the kitchen.

"Cool." Lexi tipped the bottle to her lips and dropped her head back, hoping to forget the last year of her life.

* * * *

Snow blanketed the mountains, already packing on more inches. Shoving the thick flakes from his hair, Hawk opened the door to the cabin, allowing the glow from the snow to guide him into the house.

Lexi sat with her legs hugged against her chest on the window seat. In these off moments, Lexi's vulnerability flashed louder than a neon sign. If he could demand she confide in him, he would. At the least, he'd have her tell him what was the cause of her pain that glazed over her pretty brown eyes when she thought no one was around to see it. However, women like Lexi didn't open up easily…if at all.

Drawn to the beautifully sad woman, he dumped his jacket on the seat. One by one he stripped off all the normal trappings of an office drone and made his way to her. There wasn't that much space for his big ass on the small window bench, but he managed to balance his left cheek on the edge fairly well. Wrapping his arms around her, he brought Lexi into his chest. He traced the elegant line of her neck up to her hair and took in the vanilla, coconut and pineapple that invaded his senses. *Yes,* his dick had a pathetic mind of its own, and maybe one day he would be able to control it, but the fruity scent of her hair drove him crazy.

"Want to talk about it?" he asked.

After all the kids had been put down to sleep, the wives had strolled into the family cabin. More than a smidge drunk, they had danced around singing DeBarge's *I Like It.*

Sadly, the only sober woman in the group — and against her will, he might add — had strongly insinuated that he check on his no-strings-attached friend. Always direct, he knew something was up from Remy's stern mom-tone.

"Not particularly." Lexi leaned back into him, snuggling closer. Disappointed but not surprised in her answer, he concentrated on the soft feel of her body against his. *Down, dick, down.* Always teenage-boy horny in her presence, he tried to think of something that would force his hard-on to soften.

"But you should get comfortable," she told him. "This story is going to take a minute to tell."

Chapter Twenty-Seven

The Biggie Burger Convention Center buzzed with hockey fans. Ushered backstage for the *Sports News* town hall, Hawk attempted to loosen the knot of tension that tightened his neck and pulsated between his ears. Once again stuck in a well-tailored but super uncomfortable suit, he followed the PA backstage.

Around the age of ten, the nuns had stamped that 'out of control' label no kid wanted right on his forehead. The beginning of adolescence had been a bitch for him, and those divine wives of the Lord didn't want to deal with him anymore. Who knew what would have happened if he hadn't met Knox. Apparently, his rage had been out of control to the point where the nuns had been thinking of alternative housing options for him.

In more ways than one, hockey had taught him how to hone his anger. Unfortunately, this wasn't one of those moments.

Last night Lexi had spun him a wild tale of genius, thievery and intrigue. At the end of it, he'd not only wanted to beat her ex to a bloody pulp, he'd also wanted to injure a couple of his teammates to boot. Feeling responsible for putting her in a shitty situation, he needed a spiritual release. Hawk hated the fact that he was the cause of any of her pain.

"From the scowl on your face, I don't know if this crap is a good idea or not." Marco stepped in line with him, slapping him on the shoulder.

Hawk grunted. At some point he would get his shit together, but at the moment nothing but red flashed before his eyes.

"Hey, man, can we talk?" Sven hurried to catch up with them.

"Not a good time," he replied. Hawk didn't want to sit through some fake apology. He wanted to knock the kid's head off in an effort to release some of his pent-up tension. However, at some point he would have to adult this one out.

Each team had their top players on stage for a fan Q and A. Since the Northern Royals were the champions, they would go on last.

"Look... I know we've had our differences," Sven said, "but I didn't know anything about that crap Brandi pulled. She admitted the whole thing to me, and—"

Hawk held up his hand to stop the idiot's blathering. While they waited to go on the stage, the audio people mic'd them up. Once he was through with the next hour of smiling and nodding, then he'd tell the little shit what he thought of his fiancée's stupid ass.

"Sorry," he pathetically muttered.

"Hey, hey, hey, what do we have here?" Players from the Texas Wigeons stepped in behind them.

"The team most likely to fall apart." One of the Wigeons giggled with childish glee.

"Up next," the sports announcer called. "The second-best team in the league, the Texas Wigeons."

The three clowns slid in between them.

"Let me know when you're done with that porn star, Hawthorne. I'd like a go at her."

Hawk took a step forward, but Sven jumped in front of him.

"Move," he grunted through clenched teeth.

"This is my fault," Sven admitted. "I've got this."

"And the team you've been waiting for..." the announcer geeked up the audience. "The Noo-orthern Roo-oyals!"

Screams from the crowd practically rumbled the roof off the center. Sven headed up their trio as they entered the stage. The announcer offered his hand to shake, but Sven drew back and knocked the shit out of the Texas Wigeons' captain. A shocked silence fell over the room.

"Well, fuck," Marco drawled, his southern roots spilling out. "Didn't know the Swede had it in him." No matter what they felt about Sven, there was no way they would sit back and watch their biggest competitors tear him apart.

Happy to have an outlet for all his rage, Hawk stretched the muscles in his neck and charged into the middle of the frenzy. Sinking his fist into one of the Wigeons' center's faces, he released all the frustration he'd held in since the past night.

* * * *

Opting out of anything to do with the hockey wives, Lexi decided to spend the next week with the football wives instead. The most taxing thing they'd planned was shopping and, later on, more shopping. She hadn't had any downtime since she'd taken over the bar, and this was the closet she'd gotten to a vacation in years.

Prattling around the cabin in an old tank that barely covered her breasts and teeny tiny underwear, she waited for Hawk to return from his latest marketing session. She tiptoed to the refrigerator and snatched a spoon off the dish rack.

As she pulled open the freezer, she heard the front door. Soon after, heavy footsteps followed. Grabbing the mint chocolate chip ice cream, she sank her spoon into the creamy treat.

"That was quick. I thought it would at least be a couple of—" Lexi stuck the spoon in her mouth, while she elbowed the freezer door shut. The sexy hockey player strutted into the cabin a hot damn mess. "Oh fudge," she mumbled over the mouthful of mint.

Lexi counted one black eye, a bruised cheek and a shredded tie. Hawk dabbed at his busted lip.

"It was just a bit of a thing," he told her.

"Tell me this thing wasn't about last night, was it?" Lexi reluctantly set back down her ice cream quart and went back into the freezer for ice.

Hawk peered at her through his long, loose curls that hung over his face before he swiped his hair away. In one quick motion, she snagged the dish towel from the oven's handle and rolled the cubes of ice in it.

"Sweetie, it's hockey," he said. "We fight over everything."

"Which means what?" She stepped to the towering man of muscle. Dressed to the nines when he'd walked out the door that afternoon, blood and rips decorated his designer suit.

"We don't need ammunition." Lexi gently placed the towel to his eye. "Jeesh," he hissed, but didn't move away from her touch.

"If"—she stepped closer to him, allowing his warm breath to caress her lips—"your dust-up was about me, I strongly insist you let this go."

Hawk's hazel eye twinkled under the bruises, and he lowered his lids to small slits as he put his face inches from hers. "We fight."

"But?"

"No buts." He kissed her lips, landing one soft peck then another, softly nibbling her upper lip. He didn't force his touch into a more insistent contact. Instead, he gently released her. "We fight," he murmured. "That's what we do." He laid his head on top of hers.

"There's more going on than the issue with my company and that unauthorized sex video. I can't afford for this thing to get any bigger…okay?"

A flicker of uncertainty transformed his brilliant hazel eyes to a murky brown. "Sure." He nodded. "I get it."

Lexi wanted to keep her SugarTech issues under wraps. Unfortunately, Josh's lousy-ass timing had forced her hand. Still holding the towel to his eye, Lexi kissed the corner of his lips.

"Did you need something to help with your bruises?"

"Mm-m," he groaned. Hawk picked her up and set her down on top of the kitchen counter. "I can think of a few things."

As he inched the tips of his fingers up the underside of her shirt, she put the towel of ice down and settled into his touch.

Chapter Twenty-Eight

The rest of Lexi's vacation had gone by in a relaxing but sexed-up blur. Back to the bar sooner than she would have liked, she listened to Maureen run down a list of her supposed infractions on the phone, while she monitored the main floor from her office doorway.

Of course, she'd read SugarTech's contract from front to back, but she let her lawyer blather on as she made sure no one needed a refill. Simone went for her lunch break, and her lawyer had picked that exact moment to randomly explain what was at stake for Lexi if the board voted her out.

One of the regulars crooned out a raspy rendition of *Boom Boom* that kept the small audience captivated. Remy opened the front door and jerked her head to the bar, and Lexi reluctantly nodded. She couldn't imagine a pregnant bartender being a good look.

"Why are you bringing this up?" she huffed, finally tired of her droning voice.

"Josh is trying to convince the board to convene before May."

"So, what's new? He pulls this stunt every week."

"He claims you've tried to hack into SugarTech's main server... Well, did you?" Maureen pressed, when Lexi didn't plead her innocence right away. She would have attempted to fake outrage at her lawyer's lack of confidence, but if she were being honest with herself, she would have wondered the same thing.

"Wow, no faith. If that happened, Josh would have had the FBI, SWAT or whatever branch of the government who could arrest me at my doorstep."

"That's true," Maureen muttered. "Okay, Waters, try to stay out of trouble." Her lawyer hung up without the salutation of goodbye. Sadly, Lexi had become used to her rudeness.

Whistling to herself, she practically skipped to the bar to knock Remy out of the way.

Josh was getting nervous. If the sex video had gotten out, then Lexi would instantly be in violation of her moral clause, but if Josh got the board on his side, then he couldn't be accused of revenge porn.

Grasping at straws, the little shit had apparently decided to come up with a lie that she'd hacked SugarTech's server. He had no evidence and would have most likely made something up on the fly if the board agreed to convene early.

"Having fun?" she asked her fake bartender, who went to town on the cocktail shaker in her hand.

"It was either this or a toddler tumbling class." Remy grabbed a martini glass off the back bar and poured what resembled a gimlet. Pushing the finished product to the woman who sat on the other side of the bar, she turned her attention back to Remy.

"How's Hawk?"

"Wouldn't Knox know that better than me?" Barely a day after Christmas he'd gone back on the road with his team. They had been texting, but he was too busy for much more than that.

"Hey, bro, are you okay, bro?" Remy lowered her voice ten octaves and put a dumb expression on her face. "I'm cool, dude. Cool, great. Cool. Okay, talk to you later. Bye."

Despite the mood suppressant brought on by her lawyer, she chuckled at Remy's antics. If nothing else, the woman was good for a laugh. "The coach reamed the team a new one and everyone who took part in the fight got fined."

"No suspensions?" Remy asked.

"They weren't on the ice, which helped the offenders avoid that particular punishment." Leaning against the gold railing, Lexi scanned the main floor. The bar was finally pulling in a pretty decent profit. She should have felt pleased with herself, but the aching pain that she'd somehow failed at one more thing overwhelmed every part of her.

"That's good news for Floyd Mayweather." Remy chuckled. "Now tell me the bad news, because the look on your face..." She made a circle motion with her finger and gave the best impression of a prune Lexi had ever seen.

"Shit." She was beyond tired of holding everything inside. Gliding her eyes over the customers in the room, she quietly debated with herself whether to spill her guts or not. "It's a complicated, long-ass story."

"Totally get it, but since no one's around..." She gestured toward the empty stools in front of them. The only customer had taken her drink to sit closer to the stage. "Jesus, it's hot in here."

The temperature was put at a level seventy-five degrees. Lexi snorted at her complaint as Remy shrugged out of her sweater and placed it under the bar.

"Whoa, that's better. Before you came to Chicago, I was asked to do a profile for a very popular tech company. There was lots of talk about the rise of this corporation's handsome, mysterious owner, Josh Stewart."

Suddenly thirsty, Lexi licked her lips and grabbed a bottle of water. "When—" Her voice cracked. "Uh, this assignment, when did you get it?"

"Last January."

She twisted the top off her water and downed half the bottle. That had been the month Josh had unexpectedly sprung divorce papers on her.

"A lot was coming out about how SugarTech was making waves in the industry. Josh was a regular boy wonder. No one knew anything about his private life or how he came up with so many of the apps the firm was producing."

Lexi nodded her head in agreement, since that was exactly the way he'd wanted it. Josh had claimed the anonymity would help them get a foothold in the saturated tech field.

"On the surface, Josh had the Midas touch, which definitely helped with his Machiavellian, shiny polish. The media hadn't delved too deep into the company financials or his personal life because SugarTech was on the rise with an impeccable record."

Listening for any unspoken judgment, she didn't detect any type of malice on Remy's part. Nevertheless, angry energy rumbled in Lexi's gut. She nervously tapped her nail across the top of the bar's surface. At the time, she hadn't known what changed in their relationship, but they'd been more distant than ever. Their intense work schedule could have taken some of the blame for their lack of intimacy, but in hindsight, her ex had been a shitty husband.

"Josh owns twenty percent of SugarTech, the board thirty, and a single investor named L.L. Corp owns a whooping fifty percent. Had anyone dug deep enough, they would have uncovered that Lexington Langley Waters owned L.L. Corp and was married to one Josh Stewart in his hometown of Dearborn, Connecticut."

Feeling more than foolish, Lexi nodded her head in confirmation. "He'd convinced me it would be easier to appear unattached and accessible to drum up business. While I was knee-deep in coding, he became the face of SugarTech and I missed —"

"How easy it was for him to isolate you."

Batting her eyelashes quickly, she fought to blink back the tears. "It sounds so stupid. He made it seem like he was lifting this huge weight off my shoulders. Meanwhile, he was..." Lexi shook off the depressing thought that he'd used her from the very beginning of their relationship. "The first time I went to the new office, none of the staff knew me. After the firm grew bigger and better, he moved us so far out in the valley that it became inconvenient for me to even stop by, and —"

She remembered that overwhelming, desolate feeling that haunted her throughout her entire marriage. "Josh claimed working at home would be a peaceful environment where I could create in peace." Lexi's voice broke. "God, I was so stupid."

"Sorry… I didn't mean to upset you. It's just that stunt in Aspen he pulled was brutal, and if you need any help—"

Swallowing the lump in her throat, she swatted away her concerns. "What happened to the article?"

"My editors came across a few inconsistencies in Josh's self-made story, not to mention they obtained a copy of your marriage license. Unfortunately, we couldn't get anyone to confirm his bullshit. The story was put on the back burner."

"Ahh-h, the NDA. That thing has saved his ass in more ways than I can count."

An alarm went off, and Remy checked her watch before she grabbed her sweater. "If you need anything, just give me a call."

Out of habit, Lexi swiped at the hair she'd chopped off almost a year ago with a sigh.

"Don't forget that next week is girls' night. We're having it at Dahl's restaurant."

"That's right. I finally get to see inside of that place. I hear there's a waiting list a mile-long?"

"Luckily, you know the owners," Remy replied with a smile, chucking deuces to her on the way out of the door.

Chapter Twenty-Nine

The press had ripped their team apart in the media. Sadly, it had taken the Northern Royals to show their entire ass in front of the world for them to even remotely get along better. Factoring their seven-to-one stats, Hawk's professional life was one hundred percent better. Unfortunately, his personal life did not want to flip onto the same page.

Ever since Lexi's sex tape had come to light, it banged around in his empty dome, causing havoc in his head. For all intents and purposes, he had a hard time with the thought of Lexi's ex blackmailing her. He tried to identify the span of emotions that gripped his insides, but he'd failed every time he got close to naming them.

Hatred, rage or jealousy would smack him in the face, depending on the time of day. He wasn't positive where jealousy fit into all this. He was Hawthorne freaking Maze, Northern Royals enforcer. *What the hell is this woman doing to me?*

"Aside from the full-on fiasco weeks ago, how are you guys doing?" In an odd attempt at a bro pep talk, the coach stood in front of him and Marco. Since the man was more of a bark orders, no cherry-on-top type of guy, Hawk took his question as rhetorical.

Grunting out a reply, Hawk waited for him to get on with his awkward-ass talk. Weeks on the road with no break in sight made him cranky. They always had long stretches between Canada and the West Coast during late winter to early spring months. That amount of traveling wore him the hell out.

"Fists flying is great for our brand — on ice, that is — but at a corporate event?" The gray-haired, burly dude paced the floor in front of them. Hawk had always compared his jacked-up energy to that of a caged panther. Either coach would break out of his barriers or die trying. After he'd had two heart attacks, Hawk figured the latter was on the horizon for the stressed-out former player.

"Instead of beating the hell out of your teammates, how about you veterans have a night on the town?" He stopped in front of them.

"Like a date?" Marco asked.

Hawk snorted at his question.

"What? No! I want you to—"

"Court them, wine and dine them? I got to tell you, Coach. I've never been actually asked to do this before, but hey, I'm pretty much up for anything."

Hawk didn't bother to hide his chuckle. Everyone knew Marco was bi-sexual. For the most part, nobody made a big deal out of it. Of course, the gossip from his previous team had turned into scandal, which had eventually morphed into a trade for Marco. The whole subject always seemed to make the coach a bit nervous.

"No," he sighed before spiking the tips of the plugs he had installed in his head last summer. "Go out and act like you guys are cool with each other for the tabloids." The coach turned toward the door. "We got enough bad press."

As he hurried to leave the locker room, they burst into laughter. "Why do you needle the man?"

"He's worse than my dad with the shit, and I refuse to be the only one feeling weird by the sex talk," Marco admitted.

Hawk nodded his head in agreement, even though he didn't know how it felt to have real-life parents.

Marco stood up and crossed to the lockers in front of them. "If my personal business wasn't leaked, I wouldn't get those funky, judgy vibes from everyone fifty and up."

Marco had been unexpectedly outed in a threesome with his ex-model girlfriend and the coach of some rugby league. Before anything tangible could be put out for public consumption, he'd bailed on his southern-based team.

"Got any idea what we should do with the kiddies?" Hawk asked. Sleeping was the only thing he'd planned to do. Sore and homesick, he no longer had it in him to hit the streets like he'd done earlier in his career.

Not to mention that his phone calls with the sexy most successful woman had been stilted. If he mentioned the distance, she would push off his concerns, but he could feel the chill between them. Life on the road had always come with challenges, but if Hawk were in Chicago, he was positive he could fix this weird holding pattern they suddenly found themselves in.

"One bar and that's it. Those idiots get on my nerves." Marco slammed his locker door shut with a bang. "And I don't care who knows it."

Hawk had no desire to hang out with those dimwits, but he had to at least make it look good for the coach's sake. The starters of the Northern Royals hit the overbearingly hot streets of Hollywood in search of forced fun.

"How long do we have to pretend like you two old fuckers don't suck?"

The three goons laughed.

Hawk glanced over at Marco, who raised his arms over his head to stretch. Marco's goodwill toward the mediocre amigos probably wouldn't last very much longer.

"If you fools could shut up for five minutes or less, maybe we — " Marco bitched.

The arguing began less than five minutes out of the Uber, an all-time record.

As the kiddies fought, a mile-long line in front of a restaurant caught his attention. The hodgepodge crowd was made up of baby-boomers, all black-wearing techies and millennials. "Hey." Hawk approached an older dude nearest the front of the line. "What's going here?" He hitched his thumb at the trendy brick and ivy building.

"Tech week is wrapping up. One of the major companies is throwing an after-party."

"Which one?" he asked.

"SugarTech. The CEO is throwing it."

"Invitation only?"

"Yeah, you have to get one of these." The hip, old dude flashed his phone, showing him a special invite.

"Thanks." Hawk stepped away from them, then pulled his cell out of his jean pocket. He read the name of the restaurant over the awning and texted the only person with enough pull to get him into the joint, Dahl Baby Winston.

"Guys." Once he was done, he crossed back over to the chuckleheads arguing on the sidewalk. "Guys."

"Come on, Marco. You're so uptight. What happened? Did you have a fight with your girlfriend?"

"Or boyfriend?" They laughed.

"Nah, it was your mom. We need you to move out of the house. You're cramping our style."

"What did you say?" The youngest of the Swedish crew stepped forward. Hawk grabbed his shoulder and snatched him back.

"Look, morons. We need to get into this restaurant, mingle or whatever you want to call it, then after that, we can go our separate ways."

The silly expression that generally occupied their young, dumb faces turned quizzical. "What's in there?"

"Mr. Maze?" Everyone turned toward the strawberry blonde with the walkie talkie.

"Hello, beautiful," Sven said. Unless he was looking to replace his fiancée, Brandi — which Hawk hoped like hell he did — the kid should probably keep the flirting down to a minimum.

"Follow me, please."

"Yes, ma'am." The Swedes trailed behind the hostess with their tongues hanging out of their mouths.

"That's one way to get rid of them." Marco snorted. They followed their teammates. Cutting the long line at the door, their group stepped into the restaurant.

The ivy theme continued inside. Exposed brick mixed with the bright greenery intertwined with the wrought-iron trellises. If Lexi's ex weren't the sole reason for the visit, he would have appreciated the ambiance a hell of a lot more.

The crowd instantly came off uncomfortably pretentious. Hawk hated bullshit scenes that required a fake smile and a nod. He avoided crap like this for a reason. Scanning the room, he found the tack in his shoe, Josh Stewart. The best description of Lexi's ex he could think of was tantamount to a tiny, insignificant thing. If this were the ice-skating rink, he could body check his ass into the wall then punch him silly. However, this was a civilized meeting of intellectuals, so he would need to act like he had a little more sense than usual.

Slipping his big body into the freshly empty space at the bar, he signaled for a drink while he waited for the large circle of fans that surrounded Josh to thin.

"Busy night?" he asked the bartender, once she made her way to him.

"Did these eggheads actually hire you guys to be warm-up? The tech crowd isn't that fanatical, if you get my meaning."

Hawk smiled. It figured someone at the restaurant was a hockey fan.

"Look, Missy" — he read the name off her tag — "you must have me confused with someone else. I just came here to check out the latest updates for my phone."

"After that amazing turnover to the Canadian Black Bears, I wouldn't claim those yahoos either." She nodded her head at his teammates, who were engaged in a serious game of shots across the room. He couldn't leave them alone for five freaking minutes. "What can I get you?"

"Lemonade iced tea, no sugar," he grunted.

She knocked on the wood in front of him and left him to grouse over the play that had nearly lost them the game. In short order, she came back with his drink before she moved on to the next customer.

Winning the cup had been a lifetime goal. If he'd scored that honor earlier in his career, he would probably be way worse than the newbies. Their arrogance was a problem of epic proportions.

"How are you, buddy?" Josh slapped him on the back. "That thing, that big thing worked out for you, huh?" He was half in the bag, and Hawk could tell Josh had no clue who he was. After snapping at the bartender with his fingers, he slapped his hand on the bar when she didn't answer him fast enough. "Hey, hey there, get my guy here a—"

Hawk lifted up his full glass. "I'm good, man."

"What is that, a Long Island? I thought only grandmas on cruises drank that shit." The slick guy on the lacrosse team, water polo even, laughed in his face—cute sports that would score him nothing more than a boo-boo. Josh was that rich douche who threw his weight around to score what he wanted. Hawk had met someone like him in each phase of his life, and hated every variation of the Josh clone.

"Get this man a real drink," Josh demanded. Before the bartender finished popping the top off a beer bottle, Hawk caught the 'stank' expression that twisted her face.

Tapping his hand across his head in a big, dramatic manner, he nodded with a big, goofy smile. "Now what was that thing you were working on…a movie, right?"

His schmoozy LA attitude was hard to stomach. *Did he morph into this monster or has he always been this way?* Honestly, who was he to judge Lexi's taste? His exes were the worst. *But seriously, why the hell would she be with this guy?*

"Oh, that." Hawk played along, swatting off the pretend career Josh had assigned to him. "It went about as well as expected, but I was looking to get into something new."

"Oh jah," he slurred, slipping into the vacant seat on his right. "Lemme hear it."

"Okay." Hawk swiveled in his seat toward the beach boy prick. "An app where you can send out a video and it disappears."

The silly fuck's lips twisted into smug amusement. "A few years late on that, my friend." Josh finished his drink and jiggled the Martini glass in Melissa's direction without bothering to look at her. It was a nasty, snobbish move that Hawk hated. Distracted by one of his guests who wanted to say good-bye, Josh turned away from him, which allowed Hawk to mouth 'sorry' to the bartender.

"Not like DMs, photos that disappear. I'm talking video that has no trace and deletes itself after a certain amount of time," Hawk described once he regained his attention again.

"That sounds like a tango with the FCC I wouldn't want to deal with." Josh chuckled. The bartender placed his drink in front of him, and he didn't bother to acknowledge her, let alone offer up a simple thanks. "Maybe you should stick with what you're good at — reciting those lines and smiling at the camera."

Hawk wanted to tell him the same, but only with his fist to the asshole's face. "You're probably right. Something that seems harmless could turn into an illegal tool in the wrong hands. Someone could send an unauthorized sex video. I'd imagine the FBI would have to get involved." Hawk snorted before he picked up his drink and swallowed half of his tea in one gulp. "But I don't know too much about this kind of stuff. That's more your lane." Keeping his sarcastic grin firmly in place, Hawk slipped his hand into his jean pocket. Josh was nothing more than a figurehead who had stolen and cheated his way to the top. Hawk pulled five twenties from his clip.

"Keep working on those lines, big boy. That's what they pay you the bucks for."

Laughing at the idiot's childish dig, Hawk laid the bills down on the bar.

"Yeah, it could use some work. I'll tinker with it a bit and pitch it to you again at a later date."

Hawk stood up and signaled for his teammates across the room, making his way to the door. Restraint had never been that hard to come by. Normally he could shoulder check someone into the wall and pound the anger away. However, people on Josh's societal scale didn't take kindly to well-deserved ass-whoopings.

"Enforcer!" the bartender yelled. He turned to see Melissa grab the cash. "Thanks." She held up the wad of bills. "And good luck tomorrow."

Josh's face twisted in confusion, before he leaned over the bar and pointed in his direction.

"We done here?" Marco joined him at the door. "The blondies are having too much damn fun." The Swedes had a pretty decent conga line going with what appeared to be extremely intoxicated coders.

"Yep." Hoping the sycophant Lexi divorced didn't put two and two together, Hawk stepped out of the restaurant, regretting that he hadn't punched him repeatedly.

Chapter Thirty

Lexi had noticed a pattern, although nothing in Chicago initially made sense. Chicago's loop had been coined that name due to the cable car system that circled the downtown area in the 1800s and not the famous expressway's circle interchange. The neighborhood that made up that area ranged from trendy to old ethnic eateries within the same block. Also, unlike California, where rain slowed things down to a standstill, the Windy City's tumultuous weather required people to swarm the streets at all hours of the day.

The equivalent to the happy sun cartoon singing along with the flowers made even the worse curmudgeons happy on a light rain day.

Thursdays held a nice flow of customers, but for some odd reason, Moe's was packed. Unprepared for the onslaught of bodies in the bar, they were short staffed...again. One day she would get the hang of this.

With only one server available, Lexi had to man the tables while she worked with Simone to keep up with the drink orders. They had a good rhythm down. Similar to a Broadway musical, they anticipated the other's movements to avoid a crash. Lately Moe's had been popping.

She honestly didn't know if it was the live music, Peaches' wings or Simone's eclectic drinks that were the reason for the crowds. At least the busy traffic kept her mind from drifting to parts unknown.

Managing the bar hadn't compared to the work that she loved. Lexi could create a whole world with technology, but instead, she was pouring drinks, breaking up fights or booking the next big singer. Several of her headliners had been approached by A&R people from labels or TV reality competition shows. Unlike her taste in men, apparently, she knew how to pick good talent.

For the first time since the conception of SugarTech, the quarterly meeting had been moved up. The board would be convened for an emergency meeting to vote on her future role in the company. She no longer had any faith that she could win.

Lining up the schooner like a pro, she pulled the lever on the beer tap. "Is your phone broke? Did you get a new number or what?" The harsh grumble of his voice tickled her ears.

She didn't need to look up to recognize that Hawthorne Maze was mad. It was too bad she simply didn't give a shit.

Lexi placed the glass on the bar. "Here you go, sir. Let me know if you need anything else."

"Well, now that you mentioned it." The slick suit leaned toward her.

"She didn't." Hawk pushed his big head in front of his. "Just say thank you."

"Uh, uh, thanks," the guy muttered before he grabbed his beer and left the bar.

"We need to talk."

"Busy," she said dismissively. "What can I get you, sir?" Lexi moved over to the next customer.

"A beer. He wants a fucking beer." Hawk blocked her view of the guy.

As she opened her mouth to tell the big asshole where to go, Simone squeezed her shoulder.

"I've got it. Go out back and talk."

Without another word, Lexi stomped her way to the kitchen. She had a business to run...not the one she wanted but she was still in charge. Lexi snatched the bar rag from the waistband of her jeans and threw it on the kitchen counter.

"There's my baby!" Peaches called out.

Obviously angry but not silly enough to ignore the sweetest woman on this planet, Hawk stopped at the stove to hug her. Instead of waiting for the lovefest to end, Lexi flung open the back door.

The general stink of garbage and piss didn't smack her in the face, which was unfortunate, as she could have used the funk to fuel her anger.

From the moment Maureen had called her again, she had to rein in her emotions. Robotic almost in her actions, she needed to keep everything simple in an effort not to lose her shit.

Hawk stepped out of the kitchen and slammed the door shut behind him.

"You moved out?" Hawk held his muscled body in a tight, unyielding manner.

"It was a temporary fix." She batted away his concerns with an eye roll.

"A little notice would have been nice."

"The door's fixed." She chucked her thumb over her shoulder at the shiny steel model. With a level of rage she'd never witnessed from him before, Hawk kept his hooded eyes trained on her face.

"And my calls... What's your slick reply for dodging them?"

"Well, I figured talking really wasn't our thing." Lexi slipped her phone out of her back pocket and fiddled with her screen. "Because I would have told you not to do this..." She held up her phone for Hawk to get a good view of him sitting next to Josh at a bar.

"Ah..." He closed his eyes and took a deep breath. "That's not what you think."

"Does it matter what I think. Do you care?" She waited for his reply but received nothing other than a steely stare back. "SugarTech board meets semi quarterly, but they've moved up the latest meeting to vote me off."

Raking his fingers through the long waves of his hair, he narrowed his eyes to small slits. "We were in the same town, and I popped in the restaurant where they were having a company party. The whole thing was purely coincidental. Nothing happened. Your ex left in one piece."

"That's not what Josh says. Apparently, I sent goons to harass him, and since he has that restraining order against me, I'm now in violation of our company's morals clause."

"How was I supposed to know?" he growled. "You're not exactly an open book." He shrugged his big, brawny shoulder at her without conveying one ounce of regret.

Lexi had never pegged Hawk as that guy — the take no blame, shrink away from responsibility dude. However, Moe had told her to never put people on a pedestal. They almost always displayed their entire ass and fell off that bitch.

Pissed at herself, Lexi grabbed the bridge of her nose and took a deep breath to collect the little bit of sanity she had left. "There's a ton of things that you don't know, but like every man, your ego won't allow you to step the fuck back," she said.

"Are you serious?" He lowered his face, pushing it dangerously close to hers. "If I fall back any further, I'd be off the damn cliff."

The strain of holding up her body hurt, and the burden of her problems felt too heavy to hold. Little by little the pieces of her life had come together better than the hardest puzzle to show her how truly stupid she was. "That program Josh pushed me to create...you know the one that shares video that then disappears? He claimed it would be some cute thing for parties or games."

"Look, Lexi... I don't care what the boy wonder wanted — "

She held up her hand to shush him. "Once I got it to work, he wanted me to tweak it so he could sell it off to one of his frat brothers who was a private contractor overseas. I told him no, which for me was a rare flex, but once he heard those words, the next thing I got handed were divorce papers."

Hawk's mouth moved but no sound came out. Breaking eye contact, he faced away from her. "Never have you once mentioned any of this. What? Am I too stupid to understand? Or maybe I was never good enough to share any of this with."

"Whoa." She jerked back at the hard right turn Hawk's logic had taken. "I don't know where this shit came from, but trust me, none of your psychoses gives you any right to step in and take control of my life."

"Maybe I got tired of watching you go limp."

"Oh." A slap in the face would have hurt her less. Stunned, Lexi had to shake the sting of his words off. "Is that what I'm doing?"

"From what I can tell, yeah."

"After I found his bachelor pad and smashed it to shreds, Josh got a restraining order against me. Violence isn't usually my go-to, but I was in shock — or at least that's what the dude who ran my anger management class said. How's that for limp?"

Shoving his hands in his pants pockets, he gazed at a spot directly above her head. "Not in that way," he muttered. "Look… I didn't mean to —"

"What? Insinuate that I'm weak sauce?" She tossed him a sarcastic grin. "Thanks to you, I handed Josh exactly what he wanted."

Trying to hold tough, Lexi fought off the tremble in her bottom lip and scrambled to grab the doorknob, hoping the inevitable tears that were aching to slip out didn't fall until she got far, far away from him. Lexi yanked the door open. She'd been pathetic enough for one lifetime.

Chapter Thirty-One

Nothing but the game pumped through his veins. Hawk glided across the ice, blocking his opponent's every move. Crossing one foot in front of the other, he body checked his guy into the boards. Determined to push Lexi out of his mind or the role he played in the future of her company, he snaked the puck away from his adversary. The referee blew his whistle.

"Get off my ass," the defensemen screamed before he took a swing. The hit landed against the side of Hawk's helmet. Relishing the ringing in his ears, the guy threw the next punch directly to his head.

After they grappled with each other for a second, he got the upper hand and put the dude in a headlock. Using the full force of their weight, the refs attempted to get between them, but Hawk was already in full rage mode. It took a lot more punches and blood for two more refs to yank them a part.

"Maze, out!" the ref screamed hot, angry air in his face.

He wanted to rail against the little jerk-wad, maybe even take a shot at him. However, he didn't want his career to end on such a shitty note.

"Number eighteen, Hawthorne Maze, has been put out of the game!" the announcer called over the cheering crowd. "He's been in the penalty box more this year than his whole career." Hoping to get rid of that tight grip of pain that constricted his chest every time he thought of Lexi, Hawk left the ice.

Surrounded by hateful words and boos, he walked to the locker room.

"Fucking monkey!" someone yelled from the crowd. Tired of everything in general, he slammed his hockey stick against the partition and flicked off the entire stadium. As he held his middle finger high, the cheers grew by ten. *What's one more fine?* Hawk figured.

* * * *

The streetlight beyond her window illuminated her tiny place. Lexi threw on her hoodie and looked around her apartment to make sure she hadn't left anything behind. She didn't know when she would be back. Patting down her pockets for her keys, she grabbed her travel bag and headed for the door. The vote was scheduled for the next week, but she'd decided to take a few weeks off, depending on the outcome.

Grabbing the knob, she opened the door and looked one last time. Simone had already locked up for the night. Lexi hurried down the stairs to check the alarm system, but the plunk of the piano keys made her stop mid-step.

Duke Ellington's *Slow Blues* made its way to her stairwell. Nobody but Moe could be that smooth tickling the ivories. She smiled and continued down the stairs.

The kitchen was dark. She left her travel case behind and pushed on the swinging door to the bar. At this time of night, most men his age would be in bed, but not Moe. Perhaps slower moving in every other aspect, he still played the piano flawlessly.

She crossed the hardwood floor to her dad. He didn't open his eyes when she popped a squat next to him on the bench. While his fingers worked magic on the piano, his head bobbed to the beat. He plucked the last few keys before he brought the song to a lovely, melodic end. Lexi clapped in appreciation.

"That was great. Now what did you drag your ass down here to say?"

He ripped a crusty cackle at her directness.

Moe didn't like phones. He considered music the best form of communication. Since he'd picked a mid-tempo song, she hoped this conversation would get straight to the point. "Do you remember how to play?" Moe asked.

"Very little." She hit the first chord of *Chopsticks* on her side of the piano, and he followed along. She laughed on their big finish. No one could tell her she wasn't a prodigy.

"This place." He looked around the empty bar. "I was thinking about closing our doors for good before you saved it."

"Moe's was still making money. I just gave it a little push."

"Yeah, but the fun was gone," he admitted. "My friends are getting old and sick. Nobody wants to be the last one dancing when the party's over."

That logic applied in a ton of areas in Lexi's life, her marriage included.

"The thing is you're brilliant, and the only one who doesn't see it is you," Moe said.

"Wow, this talk is turning into one hell of a morale booster." She hit the piano keys in front of her in an ominous manner.

"Yeah, afraid I was never good at that." He leaned forward, clasping his hands in front of him. "And your mom was even worse."

The unexpected jab at her mother caused an eruption of laughter to lift her spirits. The woman had never been the nurturing sort. Moe was by far the better parent of the two, which was probably the reason her mom had kept Lexi away from him. She'd claimed it had to do with those sketchy blues characters that were always around, but she knew the truth. Lexi had always preferred Moe, which meant her mother, Lorna, had made sure that no one would be happy except for Lorna.

"Did I ever apologize for that, by the way?"

"What?"

Moe tickled out an unrecognizable tune, then glided into a soft jazz song she recognized but couldn't name. "Wiggling you out of her grasp. Shit." He placed his palms on the keys, forcing a blare of clashing notes. "Josh, that little…" He blew out a breath and shook his head. "Lorna made it easy for him to slither his way into your life."

"I'm not naïve!" Lexi defended herself. "Well, not totally."

"That's not what I'm saying, but your mother made sure you knew how to work with less. Trust me when I say Josh was *much* less."

Even if he'd said anything about her ex at the time, the odds that Lexi would have listened to him were slim. "Why didn't you tell me this before?"

"Yeah." He chuckled and went back to playing the piano. "I can see it now... Hey, Lexi, that boyfriend of yours is a manipulative little turd who doesn't have one tenth of your genius." Moe tinkered with a few confusing notes before he slid into Nina Simone's *Sinnerman*. "Trust me. You would have married him even faster."

Lexi wished she could have placed blame on Lorna, but in all honesty, Josh was her fault and hers alone. Sure, she was an emotionally starved kid, but that only explained one aspect of her jumping into a pathetic-ass marriage. *What is my excuse for everything else?*

"Look, old man... None of this is your fault. You did good by me back then — and even better now." As he continued playing, she stood.

"My point," he said, finally glancing up from the keys, "is he can't take shit away from you. Anything you made, you can make again. Josh needs you — and it's never been the opposite."

Moe placed his open hand on top of the piano. Misty-eyed, Lexi placed her hand inside of his. By no means a cry baby, she'd spent this past year damn near in the fetal position.

"Hawk is a good egg. Trust me. After that last one, I would warn you off if he wasn't." As another unexpected laugh burst free from her belly, Moe squeezed her hand. "Remember, baby gurl" — he went back to playing the piano — "the only thing Josh ever won was you. From here on out, it'll be all downhill for him."

Chapter Thirty-Two

Hawk had to pay a fifteen-thousand-dollar fine, which was better than he'd imagined. However, the one-game suspension was an all-time low, even for him. Forced to sit with the coaching staff in an uncomfortable suit, he had a whole different perspective on humiliation.

Wrapping his tie around his fist, he shoved it into his pocket before he strolled through the hotel lobby. The team had a couple of days off, and he didn't need to be at practice until tomorrow. Two games into the playoffs, the Northern Royals had barely scraped by, no thanks to him. In the fight of their lives over the championship title, they needed to win the next two games.

"Hey, big guy." Hawk dropped his head back with a groan. Knox and Andre stood near the restaurant entrance. "Come on. Let's get this over with," Knox said.

Obviously one minute of peace was too much to ask. Against his better judgment, he followed them into the dining area. While he remained standing, they took a seat at the corner table.

The waitress arrived at the same time with a tray of drinks. "How long have you guys been here?" he huffed.

"Don't worry about it." Knox grabbed his bottle of beer and slid into his seat. "Hope you want nachos, because Andre already ordered a vat of them."

"When was the last time you guys flew out for one of my games?" Hawk asked, pulling his glass of iced tea closer, wishing it were a beer.

"It's been a while," Knox admitted.

"Never." Andre shook his head in disgust. "And I probably wouldn't be here now, but Knox made me come." His face twisted down while he fashioned his napkin into a bib. "Moral support or some such shit."

"Welp, you two showed support. Now get gone." Hawk nodded to the door.

"Come, come… Tell us where it hurts." Knox patted the empty chair with a chuckle.

Rolling his eyes, he pulled back the seat and plopped down.

"There's no need for a weak ass 'we're here for you' pep talk. I'm fine." He picked up the menu and thumbed through it without any real intentions or thought.

"Man, I just came to tell you how proud I am," Andre offered.

"Don't start," Hawk muttered, not in the mood for Andre's bullshit.

"No, really." He thrust his phone past Knox in front of Hawk. The video played his latest fight on the ice. "This has got to be one of my proudest" — Andre pretended to wipe away tears — "moments in our entire friendship. I mean, you finally elevated from ballerinas on skates to WWE on ice."

Despite his foul mood, he smiled. Andre couldn't be a bigger dick, but the asshole had always managed to show up for him.

"Okay, okay." Knox shoved Andre's hand out of his face. "Now that we got that crap out of the way…"

"Literally," Andre sniffed. "This is the first time I ever considered you Black."

I stand corrected. The man can be a bigger dick. Cracking his first chuckle in days, he leaned back in his chair and waved on the criticism. "Let me have it. I'm a screw-up, and why am I flushing everything I worked so hard for down the toilet, yada."

"That's not why we're here."

"Then—" The waitress dropped a huge vat of nachos on the table, interrupting them.

"Thanks," Andre said, reaching for the platter and diving in.

"This is difficult for us, but the wives—" Knox began before he reached for his beer and took a hard drag from the bottle.

"What?" He was afraid something terrible had happened, and his heart pounded in his chest. "Is everyone all right?"

"Well, not if you don't make up with Lexi."

"Huh?"

"They're going to fucking kill you."

"Is this seriously why you flew out to the middle of… Where are we?"

"Texas," Andre mumbled over a mouth full of food. "And before you say we're pussy whipped, we agree — and that's why you have to make up with her."

"Yeah, you know we don't meddle or care who you're with, but she's the only one they've liked in —"

"Ever," Andre said. "She's the only one — and trust me, man. You'd rather we give you this talk than the wives."

"My personal business isn't off limits, I take it." Hawk stared at his tea, once again wishing it were a beer.

"This is an actual quote from Remington Bell Knox." His best friend reached into his suit jacket and pulled out his phone. Flipping through his apps, he cleared his throat.

"Hawthorne Maze, Lexington Waters is the only woman smart enough, funny enough and awesome enough to win you — and most importantly us — over. If there is an ounce of regret rolling around in that big head of yours, do all of us a favor and go get her. Pretend it's one of those stupid eighties movies you love and just go."

"Well, hell," he muttered.

"Fight against that abandonment instinct...you know, that whole 'leave them before they leave you' shit that you've got going for yourself." Andre licked the nacho juice off his fingers. "Hey, should I gamble on the wings?"

"Okay, this is turning into some kind of intervention, and I'm not here for that crap." Hawk tried to put a stop to their hate fest.

"Or," Andre grunted, "should I just wait until we get back to Chicago? Also, you know you can't go to Moe's anymore because..." Andre shrugged and signaled for the waitress. "Which would be sad because that's still our hangout."

"What the hell? You only went because of me."

They nodded their heads in what he assumed was pity, although he honestly felt that Andre was still trying to figure out what he wanted to eat. He always checked out of conversations once he had his say.

"Something tells me you still have that hang-up about the smart ones," Knox said.

"Most successful," he muttered.

"Huh?" Andre grunted

"Hawk thinks they're too good for him, so he doesn't go down that avenue to begin with," Knox explained.

"Oh hell, that's why he picks the criminally stupid or just plain ole criminals. I swear the one last year lifted my Rolex off my wrist when we were playing poker." Andre showed off his watch. "This one is okay, but that baby…" He whistled low and shook his head.

"No," Hawk ground out through clenched teeth, determined to get this talk over with, "that has nothing to do with it."

"Well, you could have fooled me." Knox shrugged. "And for the record, you're too old for this crap."

"Ah-ha. I'll get some wings now, then head over to Moe's when we get back home." Andre slapped his hand on the table as if he'd discovered the answer to climate change. "Yeah, that's what's up."

Blindsided at the funky turn his life had taken, Hawk slumped farther down in his seat and groaned.

* * * *

Lexi had made the rounds in California before the big day. To lift her spirits, she'd visited Girls' Code in the tech program. They had won third place in their competition, which wasn't bad — but not the placement she'd hoped for.

Then she'd made a stop at the salon to get her hair cut even shorter. Lastly, she'd spent the rest of her time cleaning out her storage container, where she'd left reminders of her craptastic marriage. Why she hadn't set all of it on fire after the divorce, she had no idea.

Lexi waited outside of SugarTech for her lawyer. Using her highest of heels and sexiest of skirts as beautiful armor, she believed that no matter what happened, she was somewhat prepared to deal with the outcome. At least that was the lie she'd told herself.

"Early this morning, shocking." Maureen pressed the fob on her SUV while she stepped past her.

"How so?"

"To my best recollection, I don't recall you performing one single act I have requested of you."

"That's not entirely true." Lexi followed her into the revolving door of the building.

"Case in point, this emergency meeting," Maureen finished once they stepped into the lobby.

They waited for the elevator. "Keep your answers vague unless required to elaborate. This is not court, but don't give them more than they need." When the elevator cab arrived, they stepped inside. Since Lexi had nothing polite to say, she kept quiet on their short ride up to SugarTech's floor.

"If the board votes you off, we'll negotiate an exit offer," Maureen said before the doors slid open and they stepped onto SugarTech's level.

Lexi opened her mouth to point out that a little positivity would be nice but stopped in her tracks at the sight of the wives. Her feet seemed to register their presences faster than her mind. Lexi practically sprinted straight to them.

It had only been a few weeks since she'd seen them last, but it felt closer to years. They clutched each other in one big group hug. A huge wave of energy supercharged her body.

"What are you guys doing here?" she said, muffled by one of Lashonda's outrageously puffy soldier sleeves. "I thought I lost you in the divorce." She held on to them tighter, not realizing how much she'd come to rely on this bad ass gang of women.

"Divorce?" Remy asked. "But you guys weren't even in a relationship."

"Yeah, I thought you and Hawk were one very long booty call," Lashonda added.

"Of the twelve-month variety, if I am correct," Dahl pointed out.

"Okay, okay." Lexi held back a sniffle.

"Not to make this about me, but I think I've had a year-long booty call before," Dahl poked out her lip and admitted, before they burst into laughter.

"Lexi, wrap this up." Maureen snapped her fingers with a frown on her face. "We have to go."

These past few weeks had allowed Lexi a lot of time for introspection. During their marriage, Josh had managed to isolate her from friends and family, while parceling out small amounts of affection to keep her in check.

She'd allowed herself to fall for his abuser 101 schtick hook, line and sinker. There was a people pleaser aspect to her personality she hadn't realized existed until after the divorce. In a short amount of time, she'd realized people pleasing never got anyone shit.

"Go on without me."

"We're going to be late," Maureen pushed.

"Then you better hurry." Lexi hardened her tone. Cussing at her lawyer seemed wrong on so many levels — but felt totally justified at this point. Before she could let loose on a long stream of expletives, Maureen tilted her nose in the air and walked into the office.

"We wanted to wish you good luck." Dahl rubbed her shoulder.

"A phone call would have been cheaper and easier." She laughed.

"True, but we wanted celebrate your win with you," Lashonda said.

"A win? You guys have way more faith in me than my lawyer by far." Deeply grateful, she took in the faces of her friends. "Thank you for showing up. I appreciate it."

"It's nothing."

"No," Lexi said, her eyes were already watering, "it means a lot." The support she never had stared back at her from three powerfully sweet women.

"Ahh," someone cooed, as everyone came in for another hug.

"Break a leg, Hot Nerd," Remy whispered.

The pregnant wife hadn't said much. Lexi wondered what was on her mind, but she didn't have time to find out. Reluctantly, she broke loose from her cool-ass friends and headed to her proverbial execution.

Chapter Thirty-Three

Every board member was seated and accounted for at SugarTech's emergency meeting. Lexi shifted uncomfortably in her seat. Six white men, one Latino and the rest women, all white, needless to say, dissected her with their eyes across the long conference table.

Lexi had never thought about the racial makeup of the board. She'd barely attended any meeting unless a vote was needed, and even than Josh had made sure she only showed up for that in video chat.

He'd wanted to give them the impression that she was too busy creating apps to be bothered to meet with them. That meant that none of their people knew her and would not be inclined to vote in her favor. She felt the odds of keeping her board status were nil. Josh had appointed her the Wicked Witch of the West, while he'd crowned himself the all-powerful Oz.

They opened the proceedings, discussing her latest skirmishes with the law and how her actions represented the company as a whole. From across the table, Josh kept his boyish face strangely passive. She imagined him gloating on the inside.

She'd had more than a few signs in college that he was not only spoiled but lazy. He'd hidden it well with his humor and charm. Where most girls would have dumped him after they'd been conned into writing more than five term papers for him, Josh had led her to believe he would do the same for her. In all the years she'd known him, he'd never returned the favor.

"We will pass a vote on whether the company should allow Lexington Waters to stay on SugarTech's board," the acting CEO announced. Josh was the natural choice to take over as head of the company, but that had been Lexi's one and only stipulation. Instead, the board had had to appoint Josh's friend. Lexi highly suspected she was the dick in pussy type of bud to him. *Shit!* She was going to need some serious therapy after this.

Lexi held up her finger. "First, may I say something?"

"Not now," Maureen whispered, placing her hand on her leg and squeezing. "We can appeal later."

Though Maureen had come highly recommended, Lexi wondered if Josh had gotten to her lawyer. Perhaps she was paranoid. However, the douche had given her plenty of reasons to be suspicious.

The acting CEO nodded her head for Lexi to proceed.

As Josh's gray eyes twinkled in amusement, she ignored the grin that he tried to hide behind his hand. It was her ex's thinking pose that made him appear attentive rather than bored. She hated public speaking, and the fuck-stick knew exactly how much.

"Not anyone here can say we're perfect—"

"Oh hell," Maureen muttered.

"Unfortunately, people often behave illogically under high levels of stress. I went through one of the most stressful times of my life last year, and I may have made some rash decisions." Lexi kept steady eye contact with each board member. Failing to skip over Josh, she caught his eye roll, which caused her to stutter.

"Last year was just a small example of your inability to lead this company." Josh seized the moment to take over the floor. "But your behavior of late is the reason you should be removed from the board all together."

The sheer sound of his voice caused Lexi's hand to involuntarily twitch. Direly wanting to bash his face in, she intertwined her fingers together and lowered them into her lap.

"As I was saying," she announced loudly, cutting him off. "This room is filled with brilliant businessmen and women who have made a misstep or two. If I'm not mistaken, there's a couple of DUIs in the room and a few lawsuits of the paternity sort." Lexi noticed the frowny faces and the nervous leg jitters from the men in the room, but she didn't care. Who were these people to judge her?

"Stop," Maureen hissed under her breath.

"But what I'm positive no one has questioned is your right to be in the room, much less be invited to the table—especially the one you single-handedly built."

"If that's all, Ms. Waters." The acting CEO cleared her throat. "May we vote?"

"Finally," Josh sighed.

* * * *

Lexi's heartbeat thundered in her ears. She continually stabbed the button to the elevator with her finger but got nothing. As the nervous energy pumped her up, she settled for the stairs to work off her adrenaline. She took two steps at a time. Without breaking her neck, she landed on the last floor, thankfully feet first, and shoved open the lobby door.

Huffing out of breath, she frantically looked for the girls but didn't see them. *Did they make plans for later?* She couldn't remember whether they were sticking around or not. Her thoughts were bouncing around a thousand miles per hour.

"This isn't over," Josh growled. Snatching her by the arm, he pushed his face close to hers.

"Wow, when money is on the line, you move fast. What did you do, take the stairs or hop on your broom to fly down here?"

"Laugh now, but when I get my company back, you won't be finding shit funny."

"According to that vote" — she yanked her arm out of his grip — "you don't *have* a company."

"You may have made a couple of codes," he spat, "even started the initial process, but this is my blood, sweat and tears. You wanted to create websites, for fuck's sake!"

Josh's gray eyes turned a wicked shade darker. *What the hell did I ever seen in him?* His sweet mask of goodwill slipped away, leaving the petulant child who had squatted inside of him baring his teeth at her.

"Look... Look..." Running his hand through his chestnut hair, he turned away. When he faced her again, he'd schooled his expression into a tight smile. "We can work something out. I mean...I'm sorry. This doesn't have to be over." He grabbed her hand.

Completely shocked by his Jekyll and Hyde impersonation, she jerked away from his touch.

"Are you serious?" No longer disillusioned that Josh wasn't always a monster, she considered breaking into a run.

"Hear me out. We just hit a rough patch. Every married couple does."

"A rough patch," she repeated, confused by his utter lack of self-awareness.

"This was a bump," Josh continued his bullshit. He closed in the space between them as he clasped her shoulders. "Why would we throw eleven years down the toilet without a fight?"

Delirious with the twist and turns from the day, she bowed over with laughter. "Good question." She petered off with a hiccup. "Probably because you tried to mentally break me down and embarrass me in front of the world. Oh, and that was only after you took every dime I had to my name."

"Don't exaggerate." He pursed his lips in a tight line.

Bored with the conversation, she glanced around for an official out. "I wish I was." The girls stood waiting for her in front of a black SVU. Lexi attempted to walk around him, but Josh tightened his hold on her.

"Taking you down won't be hard." He fixed his face with that slick smile that had always gotten him everything he wanted. Of course, it was only for the public. Lexi knew if they were alone, he'd be losing his shit. "Don't forget. I still have that video of us." He puffed his hot coffee-fetid breath in her face. "And I'm not above using it."

"Good talk." She shoved him in that soft spot right under the chest plate.

"Oooof." He stumbled back, and Lexi hurried passed him. "Enjoy this little victory, baby, because when I get through with you..." he huffed, out of breath.

While they waited for her to join them, the girls did a little dance with humps and thrust. Crude didn't quite cover their moves, but it was adorable, nevertheless.

"Josh Stewart?" Lexi peeked over her shoulder when she heard the full use of his name. Two officially dressed men approached him, flipping out their badges. "We're going to need you to answer a couple of questions for us."

"What's this about?" He straightened up to his full height.

"An unauthorized video. We were hoping you could clear up a couple of things." Stopping in her tracks, Lexi turned all the way around to witness the agent place his hand on Josh's arm.

"We won't be going anywhere without my lawyer," Josh demanded.

"Not a problem, Mr. Stewart." They steered him toward their vehicle. "Your attorney can meet us at our office."

"What? No." Josh struggled against the tight box they maneuvered him into. "I want him now."

"Call him from the car."

Lexi's eyes connected with Josh's before the agents placed him in their SUV and winked because...*Fuck Josh. That's why*.

"Oh wow, that was better than dodgeball," Remy cooed. The wives surrounded her in one big huddle.

"How were you able to − ?"

"We had Tanya save the video on her phone with the help of a really good hacker. She traced the original sender of the app and the server where Josh kept the video stored."

"So, is that why you came?" Lexi confronted the three biggest instigators.

"Besides supporting you?" Dahl nudged her with her shoulder. "Yes, we totally wanted to see that."

"Live and in person." Lashonda smiled bigger than she'd ever seen before.

"Also" — Remy reached out to fix the neck of Lexi's long sweater — "remember how we made you watch *Flashdance* for girls' night?"

"Uh yeah." She drew out the words. "And it sucked."

"That movie is a whole college semester in problematic eighties films," Remy told her, waving her opinion off. "But, it's also his favorite." She grabbed her arms and turned her in the opposite direction. Three cars down, Hawk leaned against an old pickup truck, holding peach roses and a puppy. Instantly, the sight melted her heart.

"To tell you the truth, I think it's because the lead was bi-racial like him. I mean, otherwise, it doesn't make a whole lot of sense," Dahl admitted.

"Don't forget the boobs," Lashonda added. "It's always the boobs."

"Go ahead. You know you want to." Remy shoved her in the direction of the damned cutest thing she'd ever seen. "And act like you weren't drunk when it was on and play along."

As she approached him, Lexi ignored the fluttering in her stomach. Butterflies couldn't hold a candle to the Flock of Seagulls going nuts inside of her…the band, not the birds. Big and bronze, his muscles rippled under his denim shirt.

Hawk had tied his wavy hair back in a ponytail, which drew out his strong bone structure. Fighting off a full-blown smile, she stopped in front of him. "Are those for me?" His hooded eyes roved over her body, landing on her face. He passed the roses to her. "And…" She tried to grab the furry booger in his arms, but he pulled the puppy out of reach.

"The dog's mine." Hawk chuckled.

"But in the movie, it was Alex's."

"If you remember, she also gave him a rose back," he said.

Lexi plucked a flower from the bundle and passed it to him. When he accepted it, she bit her lower lip at the adorableness overload.

"How did it go?" Hawk asked. His deep voice was extra gravely. Resisting the urge to touch the slight shadow on his face, she clasped the wrapping around her roses even tighter. Regardless of his natural bedraggled beauty, he seemed exhausted.

"Like you don't know," she poked.

With a slip of a smile, he raised his hazel eyes skyward before he returned his gaze back to her face. "Pretend that I don't."

"Ah." Lexi felt suddenly shy but mainly uncertain. She shifted from one high heel to the other. "They had the vote. I didn't think I stood a snowball's chance of winning. Then a miracle happened, and the oldest most curmudgeonly board member voted in my favor. Who knew Frank Stolley was a hockey fan?"

The corner of Hawk's full lips turned up, and he ducked his head. "He's not… Sports aren't really Frank's thing."

"So, my boyfriend —"

"Your what?" he prodded with a teasing smile. He raised his eyebrow, most likely waiting for her to elaborate.

Instead of repeating herself, Lexi sucked her lips into her mouth, hoping the earth wouldn't open, swallowing her whole.

"Before I 'fess up, let me start with this," he said. "I'm sorry. I shouldn't have interfered in your business with Josh." Hawk flipped the puppy around, forcing the furry monster to hypnotize her. "In the past, I've never had to ask."

"There's no way I'm the first woman you've met who's not interested in the Flintstones' guide to relationships." Lexi snorted.

"Not what I meant. Sheesh." He blew out a ragged breath and shoved a loose curl away from his face. "I should have been straight and told you I wanted an exclusive relationship instead of tiptoeing around the subject. I didn't have any right to interfere with you and your company."

"Which you apparently did again." Lexi nodded at the office building behind her.

"Only to fix my initial fuck-up. I thought I would have to pull out every trick, but Frank and I had a two-hour conversation about his time in Vietnam."

"And during this 'bro chat' you just happened to mention Josh's plans if he got control of the company," she pushed.

"His college ties to private contractors overseas may have come up. I honestly can't remember."

No words passed between them as they stared one another down. The few weeks they had been apart, she'd missed him terribly, but felt her neediness was one more character flaw she would have to address.

"Anyway, this might be a little late in coming, but do you want to be exclusive?"

The ridiculous amount of cuteness in front of Lexi tugged at her heart strings. She shyly smiled at the big man holding a puppy and nodded her head.

"There's not a chance you'll break up with me after recess, will you?"

The nervousness that had gripped her from the time she woke up until the board meeting finally dissipated within her laughter. "Depends on where you take me for lunch."

"Well, in that case, do you want to road trip with me to Canada to celebrate your win?"

Shocked that she'd forgotten about the playoffs, Lexi's covered her mouth with her hand. "Oh, Hawk, I'm sorry. How bad was it?"

"We managed to keep up until game five, then the rest of the series was pretty tragic."

Feeling bad about his loss, she drew her lips down into a pout.

"We'll get them next year." He stepped closer to her. "Now what do you say about Canada?"

"Hmm-m." She nodded toward the puppy. "May I?"

"Yeah, but you have to give her back."

While he passed the puppy over, Lexi did a little dance in place. "What's her name?" Bright blue eyes stared back at her as she grabbed the cutie and nuzzled their noses together.

"Haven't picked one yet."

She studied her closely. The furry black-and-white beauty tilted her big head to the side. "How about Storm from *X-Men*?"

"That's too on the nose. We'll split the difference and call her Stormy."

"That's sort of pornish, but okay." Lexi lifted her higher above her head. "Hey, Stormy, I'm going to make you love me."

Lowering his head, Hawk grabbed her by the waist and kissed her. Hard and sweet, he moved his lush mouth against Lexi's. The puppy struggled to work her way into their lip lock. "Trust me," he murmured when he pulled away from her lips. "That won't be hard."

Chapter Thirty-Four

Three months later

They had bumped around Canada for a month, then settled at his house. It was a work in progress. A million things on it still needed to be done, but nevertheless it was the closest thing he had to a real home.

Patiently he waited for Lexi to take Stormy out. Hawk counted to ten before he jumped out of the bed.

Less than four years before, he'd bought an acre on Knox's family's land. Construction on his house had been slow going but they were almost done. Hurrying to grab the champagne flutes out of the closet that he'd stashed there an hour ago, he set them on the nightstand. The third step on the stairs alerted him that his time was up. *Dammit, Stormy!* The runt usually took much longer to explore her territory, but apparently time wasn't on his side.

When he had showed up to SugarTech's offices three months before, he'd been willing to beg her to take him back. He couldn't remember ever chasing after anyone, but their blow-up had made him realize how good they were together.

Of course, the girlfriend bar was super low in that area, but she made him happy. Not that he needed Lexington Waters to make him happy, but there was no one on this earth he would rather be happy with.

Hawk pulled opened his nightstand drawer and dug under his infinite number of T-shirts. He popped the diamond into his mouth as she pushed the half-cracked door open.

"She didn't want to get off the porch." Lexi put the fat furball on the floor.

Hawk admired the way his college jersey fell to the middle of her milk chocolate legs. She pushed her glasses farther onto her face and nudged the ridiculously cute pup with her foot.

Nervous, he tucked the ring inside of his cheek.

"What's this?" Lexi accepted the bubbly drink from him before she bounced on the bed.

"Celebration." He tried not to choke. "Our anniversary."

"Three whole months, eh?" She snorted. "That's Canadian speak." Lexi tucked her legs underneath her and winked at him when he handed her a full flute.

"We've been together a year, but we finally got our shit together three months ago."

"I'll drink to that." She clinked her glass into his and raised it to his lips. He gently covered the mouth of her flute.

"That's not the toast."

"Oh, okay." She rolled her hand, signaling for him to wrap it up.

"Shit," he hissed. What did he know about anything romantic? Shoving his hair back, he settled on the first thing that came to mind. "Marry me."

Lexi opened her eyes wide in shock. They never discussed it before, and he didn't even know if she wanted to get married again.

"Whaaa—?"

"The new season is coming up, I leave for camp in a couple of days, and…" He swallowed this hard lump in his throat and hoped it wasn't the ring.

The silence that encompassed the room felt all-consuming. Of course, Stormy picked that moment to whine. Instead of answering him, Lexi turned around and picked the little cock blocker up from the floor. It felt like an hour had passed since he'd blurted out his word salad of a proposal.

"That was a lot," she admitted, clutching the puppy to her chest. "So you want to marry me because you're going off to camp?" Squinting her big, brown eyes at him, her pretty doll face held that analytical 'thinky' expression. His stomach twisted into a bow, then tightened into one hell of a knot.

"No. Shit, I'm bad at this." He pulled the ring from his mouth. "Because I want to spend a couple of lifetimes loving you."

"How long did you have that in your mouth?"

"Is that your answer?"

"No. I mean, my answer is 'yes'." The ends of her lips curled up, raising her cheeks even higher. Lexi put out her hand. Grateful, he slid the sparkler on her finger. Slipping his hand around the back of her slender neck, he brought her lips closer.

"Cool, you want to do it today?"

"Huh?" She pulled back before he could seal the deal with a kiss.

"It's just that with the new season starting, I wanted my good luck charm with me." Feeling he was losing his nerve, he sat up, forcing the sheet to slip off his lap. "Hey, eyes up here."

Lexi glanced at his groin and licked her lips with a wink. "If you can pull of a wedding today, then I'm all in," she huffed, falling across his chest.

"For real?"

"My day is free. Why not?" He snatched her little body up to his lips, kissing her whole face. Mad to be left out of the fun, Stormy hopped up and down on the bed, puppy barking her displeasure.

"Are the courts even open today?"

"No." He stood up, tugging the sheet from underneath her to wrap it around his body.

"Hey!"

"Sorry," he chuckled. He crossed the room, then opened the bay window.

"What did she say?" Andre yelled. Hawk's whole gang stood outside of the house, waiting for Lexi's answer. They'd promised they would arrive a little past dawn, and they'd actually kept their word. Of course, it didn't help that Andre held a sign that read, 'Say no'."

"You're a real shithead, Dre," he yelled down.

Lexi jumped off the bed to join him.

"What the hell?" She threw a confused wave at the crew.

"If you'd said no, we were just going to have a barbecue at the house," he explained, "while I got drunk and pouted for the rest of the day."

She held up her left hand, showing off her ring. "Let's throw a wedding!"

As everyone cheered, he flicked off Andre, who dug into his pocket and passed over a roll of bills to his wife.

Knox had built a house on the farm next to his parents. Once they combined the land, there was enough left over for four more homes and a baby golf course. Since Hawk considered the Knoxes his family, he'd bought the neighboring lot to be closer to them. Not only did Lexi love their bond, but the property was a sight to behold.

The guys were pressuring Andre to join their trifecta to make it complete and buy an acre. She didn't think they'd convinced him...yet.

After working through the initial shock of Hawk's proposal, Lexi had been whisked to Remy and Knox's Tudor home. It was designed in a fairytale manner that the family used for summers and Christmas holidays.

While she got glam for an impromptu wedding, the women flitted all around her. Lashonda had brought several dresses for her to choose from. After she picked one, they'd quickly tailored the gown to fit her.

Lexi had never had a wedding before. When she'd gotten hitched to that treacherous leech, they had gone down to the courthouse for one of those quickie numbers. No family or friends, and the whole thing had been over in less than ten minutes.

Holding Remy's brand-spanking-new baby girl in her arms, Lexi cooed at her as the stylist curled sexy waves in her hair. Everything had been planned to a type-A degree. There was nothing for her to do but sit back and let everyone take care of her, "or be slapped silly", which had been Remy's exact words. Nails, hair and makeup technicians waved their fairy wands around her to make everything perfect.

Once she'd finished dressing, classical music played over the PA system. Lexi downed the rest of her mimosa before she took her spot at the back of the wedding party.

The Knox family had decorated their backyard with millions of candles and exotic flowers. A million may have been a smidge of an exaggeration, but it really did seem like a magical fire hazard.

How a wedding had been assembled in such a short amount of time she had no idea. Yet, she'd never been happier in her life.

The sun slipped under the horizon, coloring the world in brilliant purple hues. At the end of the aisle, Hawk stood in the white gazebo waiting for her. James Bond had nothing on this man. His tux fit his muscled body impeccably. He'd pulled his long waves into a bun.

Hawthorne Maze was hot as hell.

"Glad you two finally got your shit together." Moe met her at the French doors.

"Pops!" She nearly melted at the sight of her old man. She threw her arms around him and held him close.

"Amazing." He pulled back to admire her dress. Lexi had chosen a sleek, beaded 1920's sweetheart bodice that hugged her body all the way to the floor.

The music changed from a recorded selection of Johann Sebastian Bach's *Air* to live blues. Recognizing the arrangement of Louis Armstrong's *What a Wonderful World* right away, she peeked outside. Pops' band had assembled on a stage not too far away from the gazebo. "Dad, did —" Stuck in the muck of her own drama, she hadn't put much thought into the next few minutes of her life, let alone her future. "Hawk asked you for my hand?"

"A while back." Moe chuckled. "Never thought he'd seal the deal this quick. Hawk's usually the 'beat around the bush' sort."

"Pretty much," she muttered.

"Well, shall we?" He offered his arm. Lexi slipped her hand into the crook of his elbow as they set off down the aisle.

Nothing could steal her attention from Hawk. His tawny skin glowed under the remaining rays of the sun. Mesmerized by the sexy-ass man in front of her, she almost missed her father kissing her cheek and leaving them alone.

"Wow," he said. His warm hazel eyes softened when she took his hands.

As the magistrate read their vows, she burst into a peal of church giggles that couldn't be controlled. "What?" he whispered, arching his eyebrow.

"I'm just happy."

"Yeah?"

"Uh-huh." She nodded, holding in a snort. "I'm happy I didn't fire you."

Getting lost in a world of their own, they both giggled at the irony of it all.

Chapter Thirty-Five

They had moved the wedding party to the back of Knox's childhood home for the reception — a whimsical setup that incorporated nature seamlessly in their theme. The fir trees along the property were twinkling with lights, while floating candles covered the sky. Fire hazard once again crossed her mind, but she got lost in the dreamlike quality of the day. Honestly, she couldn't have planned it better herself.

Most of the old-timers had headed off to the hotel after they'd cut one of the six cakes that layered the table. The wives and Hawk's teammates had stuck around, enjoying the bar and crazy popular DJ late into the night.

Ting, ting, ting. Knox tapped his fork against his glass. "Best man here wants to make a toast." Relaxed and laid back, all the men had taken off their suit coats. A lot of oily, hard muscles rivaled the glare of the candles that burned well into the night.

"Wait," Andre said. "First, I'm going to need that DJ to dip his ass on out of that booth."

"He's a top ten DJ," Hawk groaned.

"Yeah, well, he's playing shit." Andre shimmied his ass over to the booth.

"Leave him alone and sit your ass down," Hawk demanded.

Hawk was more chill than she'd ever seen him, and Lexi didn't want to change the trajectory of the day. Draped on her Hulk of a man's lap, she placed her wineglass down on the table next to her and sat up. Rubbing her hands together, she was all set to solve their first martial problem.

"Dre," she yelled. "DJ Boom."

The kid's rigid stance told her he was ready to go to blows with Andre. The guy looked no older than an eighth grader.

"Yell out which one you prefer...*Champagne Supernova* or *Wonderwall*?"

Andre scrunched his face up. "*Wonderwall*," he cried, throwing his hands up.

"Clearly *Supernova*," the DJ replied.

"Dre," the crew yelled.

"Traitor." Hawk nibbled on her ear.

"Now can I toast?" Knox huffed. His wife patted her husband's back with her free hand as she rocked the baby to sleep. Considering she'd pushed out a seven-pound human being less than a month before, Remy appeared every bit a Mother Earth goddess. Gloriously perfect in their silver gowns, her bridesmaids struck one hell of a stylish pose.

"To my best friend, Hawk." He raised his glass. "I love you like a brother and I never thought you would find someone who could be any sort of match for you.

Lexi, you make our gang complete. Dahl and Bane, you are the sweetest of us all, whether you want to admit that or not." He mentioned the couple who sat near the edge of the lawn. "Of course, me and Remy are the sexiest."

"Damn right," Remy cosigned him, to drunk laughter.

"And you two are the cool ones. All our partners are the halves we needed, and I'm just happy you guys found each other to make it complete... Congratulations."

"Congratulations," everyone followed.

"Hey, what about me and Shonda?" Andre yelled.

"Damn, man, I was trying to keep it sweet, but—"

"Crazy!" Hawk screamed back. "You two are the freaking crazies."

"Nooo," Lashonda yelled, while searching the faces of everyone left in the crowd. "Okay, whatever." She waved them off.

"Thanks." Hawk turned toward Lexi, nuzzling the crook of her neck.

"For?" Wrapping her hand into his curls that had escaped his bun, she pulled him closer to kiss the edge of his lips.

"Accepting this makeshift family, me—and most of all for being you," he murmured. Even though she was immersed in the soft feel of his lips, his words finally caught up with her dreamy state of mind.

"Crap!" She pulled away from Hawk, frantically looking around the yard. "Time! Does anyone have the time?"

"Five a.m.," someone called out.

Lexi swung her legs off him and stood. She walked to the end of the lawn that had a good view of the road between the properties.

"Babe?" Hawk called behind her.

The sky had turned a fire orange from the sun rising. Lexi had missed its initial arrival.

"Ah, promise you won't be mad." The houses were located off a dirt road. If anyone came toward the property, she would be able to see them.

"Today you have an unlimited pass." He wrapped his arms around her body.

"Good, because I found your birth dad and he's supposed to be coming, like soon."

"Here?" Suddenly weightless, Hawk picked her up when he flipped her around to be nose-to-nose with him. "When?"

"Um, this morning. I meant to tell you yesterday, but then we got married and the day got away from me..." Lexi petered off as a myriad of expressions changed his handsome face. Confusion seemed to be the main one he settled upon before she continued. "Since I didn't know how open you would be to the whole thing, I asked Knox to talk to him...with me."

Hoping she would receive an assist from Hawk's best friend, she looked over his shoulder, scanning the yard. Knox was nowhere in sight. Her eyes landed on Remy. "Baby brain."

"That doesn't apply for men!" Hawk hollered.

"Dads go through it too, you know."

The jarring sound of a needle off the record ripped through the uncomfortable silence. "And you thought we were the crazy ones." Lashonda leaned against her husband with a smug smirk.

Hawk touched his finger to her chin, moving her face back to his eyeline. "Ever since the kids, Knox's been a flake. I'll deal with him later. Now, what the hell?"

"It was a puzzle that I thought I could crack by myself, and when I couldn't, I enlisted Remy's hacker friend."

"Bumblebee," he muttered.

"Yeah. It took a while, but we found your bio dad...an African American teenager who got an Indigenous girl pregnant. They ran away to Canada thinking they would get married, but her family caught them before that happened. There's more to the story, but he should probably tell you."

"And what time exactly is this meeting supposed to take place?"

Brighter than it had been moments before, the sun completely crested over the horizon, and Lexi caught the sight of dirt kicking up behind a minivan at least a half mile down the road. "About now."

Hawk dropped his head back with a sigh.

"If you want to meet them alone," Remy said, "we can get out of your way."

"No, no." Hawk stepped away from the group and closer to the edge of the yard. "I meant what I said. We're family, and I want you guys to stay." He held out his hand for Lexi. She joined him facing the road. "This is actually perfect timing."

"Yeah?" Lexi twined her fingers between his.

"Yeah," Hawk affirmed. Lifting her hand to his lips, he brushed them against her skin before he sweetly kissed her. "It couldn't be better."

Epilogue

One solid season had passed and the Northern Royals had won the playoffs. Hawk stood outside of his favorite bar clutching the Keating Cup within his grip. He honestly couldn't remember a time where everything in his life had come together this perfectly, and it all had begun with Lexington Waters-Maze.

Hawk grabbed the handle to Moe's and pulled the door open. When he peeked his head into the bar, cheers rocked the room. He did a quick scan of the crowd. "Where's Lex?"

"Not here yet, but…" Not bothering to listen to any excuses, he ducked out. Cries of disappointment filtered their way outside.

"Come on, Hawk. She's on her way!"

"I'm not coming in until Lexi's here." A curse word or two made it to his virgin ears, but Hawk wouldn't be moved. He leaned against the door and waited. Of course, it didn't help that a group of fans was taking pictures of his immature stance from across the street, but he wouldn't be deterred.

"Hey!" Lexi hung out of the window of the Uber she was in. "Sorry... My flight was late." For the past year she'd flown back and forth from her California offices and the bar. Lexi had kept Chicago as her home base while she made it to the quarterly meetings. Hawk had had no problem moving to the West Coast once he retired, but Lexi had declined his offer. She enjoyed her Chicago family too much to uproot them.

Not to mention his bio dad lived in Wisconsin, which made it easier for them to visit. Unfortunately, he hadn't been able to track down his mom. The story went that after her family had kidnapped her to Canada, his dad never saw her again. Lexi and her girl gang of tech wizards were working on her trail. Until then, he had done a pretty good job melding his bio family with his adoptive one.

Within weeks of his wedding night, he'd been introduced to a couple of siblings who didn't mind learning about hockey—even though Andre swore they were merely humoring him.

"Why aren't you inside?" Lexi yelled through the car window. Hawk met her at the door and brought her pouty lips to his, kissing her silly before she could get out.

"We went over this... I go into the bar and you yell 'surprise'." She ducked her head back into the window of the Uber.

"But I'm out here with you, so why don't we just walk in together?" He opened the door to the sedan and grabbed her bag from the driver as he hoisted the cup onto his hip.

"Because I saw this whole thing in my head. You at the front of the crowd cheering me on with my new family and old one."

"But…" Determined to get his way, he arched his eyebrow and frowned. It would be the only sign to her that he wouldn't budge.

"Fine." She sighed on her way to the alley. "But sometimes I think Dre is right about you."

"No, no, no," he shouted at the back of her head, paparazzi be damned. "My wife, my side."

Annoyed at the delay, he signed a couple of autographs and took a couple of selfies. "Okay!" Lexi yelled from inside.

Balancing the cup and her bag, he opened the door to lackluster cheering. "Do better or I'm walking right back out that door again."

"Yay," they applauded uproariously.

"Okay, fine." He entered the bar with a snort. Hawk made the rounds with his cup. Unlike the last time, he had invited one team member — and thankfully, Marco had shown up.

"Congratulations," Bernard Bueller said. His dad looked young for his age. He had a head full of salt-and-pepper hair, dark brown skin and very few wrinkles. Hawk hugged his dad and slapped his two brothers' hands. Younger than him by five years, both kids had more of a slender built but matched Hawk in height.

After the wedding, Bernard had told him about his mom. Teenagers at the time, she'd gotten pregnant with him and they made plans to meet up in Canada. However, she'd never showed. Bernard had no idea what had happened to her or Hawk. He'd gone into the military, and when he'd gotten out, he'd searched for his mom, Leilani, but had come up with nothing.

"This is a nice place. I see why you come here. Oh, and we met Lexi's dad." He pointed toward the stage where Moe was jamming out with his band. Since Lexi had started the live entertainment, her father and his friends had gotten their mojo back. They planned on cutting new music, then going out on tour. To say he was proud of Moe was an understatement.

"Hey, Hawk's fam, how did you like football players' ice capades?" Andre laughed, while he slipped in the middle of their circle. He wrapped his arms around his brothers' shoulders.

"We love hockey," Stephen, his youngest brother, admitted.

"Almost more than skiing," his middle brother chimed in.

"But our favorite is curling," the family said in unison.

"Okay." Andre's slick smile disappeared from his boy-band face. Hawk could tell he was at a loss for words, which rarely happened to the former football player. Unwrapping his arms from around them, Andre left their little group without another word.

"That was the best present ever." Hawk pretended to dab at his eyes. It almost made up for all those years he'd dealt with Andre's bullshit.

"Huh, I didn't think that would actually work. What's curling?" Stephen said.

"That guy is my kid's favorite football player. Do you think I should tell him?" the middle brother offered.

"No, no, no," Hawk warned them, close to stamping his feet like a child. "Don't ruin this for me." Andre was already mad that he'd introduced Bane's foundation to winter sports. This little joke had made Hawk's entire night.

"That was fun, but I need to go to the little boys' room," Bernard announced to the group. He hopped off the tall stool and made his way across the stuffed bar. Hawk hadn't gotten around to calling him 'dad'. He wasn't quite there...yet. Hopefully, it would be easier once some time had passed.

"Hello, family," Lexi said, joining them.

"When are you going to give us some nephews?" Stephen patted her shoulder.

"Get out of my uterus, sir!" Lexi yelled. She hollered over the bar's noisy chatter. It quieted down enough for them to hear a tinkle of laughter in the background, as Stephen yanked his hand away from Lexi.

"Dammit." Hawk swiveled his head around the bar to look for the offending party.

"My night, my wife, Requiem Knox. You promised best behavior."

"No such thing," she huffed somewhere nearby.

"Warning you, lady Knox, I will snatch my baby out of this town before your next dodgeball game."

"You wouldn't." He hoped that threat got through to Remy. Her behavior was almost worse than her silly-ass husband's.

"Watch me!" he hollered. Lexi had kept Remy's team on top. If he took her away, then the Ladybug's championship title would be in dire jeopardy. "What was that about?" he asked his nutty wife, who could never pass up on one of Remy's little stunts.

"She bet me that one of you would ask about kids, but I told her there was no way a group of dudes would care. Soooo—"

"Let me guess, if they did, you were supposed to yell out crude shit." Hawk pulled her closer to his side to plant a kiss on top of her head. "Stop playing with that crazy lady."

"Can we get a photo of the family and the cup?" a reporter interrupted them. Hawk had allowed a few journalists in the bar this time around.

It was his last year, and he didn't want to be bombarded with a lot of 'what's next for the enforcer' questions. Hopefully, they would pop out a couple of kids, but he didn't want to put too much pressure on Lexi. She had her CEO position and had begun the heavy task of moving SugarTech to Chicago.

A little while after Josh had been slapped with probation and community service, he'd tried to wiggle his way back into the everyday swing of the company, but he'd been banned from the premises and forced to respect the non-compete order if he wanted to keep any of his stock options. That was a win-win for everyone in Hawk's book.

Other than spending time with family, his only plan was to help Bane's foundation. He'd already told them as much, and unfortunately the vultures would offer him unsolicited advice on what to do after hockey. It seemed to be a game between the sports reporters to see which one could make him snap the fuck out the fastest. Since he didn't plan on dealing with them anymore, he'd allowed only a handful of the vultures to attend his day with the cup.

"Sure." Hawk waved everyone over. The usual suspects crammed in next to him.

"We meant your immediate family," the reporter said as Lexi hugged his waist along with the guys he grew up with, their wives and his biological peeps crowded all together.

"This is my immediate family. Now take the damn picture."

"All right, on three," the reporter said. "One...two..."

"Champions!" everyone yelled.

Want to see more from this author?
Here's a taster for you to enjoy!

Spies R Us
Amber Malloy

Excerpt

Spring was directly around the corner, which would conclude the twins' first year of preschool.

Vann idled at the kids' school in the carpool lane at the kid's school. He waited for the kids with Dylan Hansen, his best friend, in the passenger seat. Dylan had been a one-time silent partner in Vann's environmental investment firm, Good and Green. However, after this last quarter, Vann had been able to buy him out.

"They're late," Vann said, checking the clock on the pickup's dashboard. The little ones always got released first.

"Why don't you go check on them? That group of women over there are gobbling me up with their eyes, and it's making me feel naked."

"What?"

Dylan nodded toward the housewife gang and joked. "Unlike you, I'm not damaged goods. A runaway wife and two kids. I, on the other hand, am a shiny nugget of gold." Dylan chuckled as he pointed at himself. "Single and divorced moms can sniff me out a mile away. I think it's a sixth sense they acquire the minute they sign their names on the divorce papers."

Vann didn't doubt what Dylan said. The women were oftentimes overly friendly. He always wondered if it had to do with his semi-single status, but on the other hand, someone baggage free like Dylan would be prime beef.

"If you'd just divorce Eden, then you too could be held in high regard, such as I am." Dylan ran his hand through his blond hair and polished his fingers on his shirt. Friends since college, they were often mistaken for brothers. Yet ever since Vann had let his hair grow past his shoulders, Dylan appeared the more desirable of the two.

The mandatory uniform at Vann's company ended with jeans and began with a T-shirt — preferably clean, but that requirement wasn't always met. Once he'd shed his jacket and tie, the fairer sex had begun to migrate toward men with a more grown-up look. Jobless or homeless seemed to be the popular opinion about his life. Apparently neither of those options qualified him as good husband material, though they still seemed to look at him hungrily.

"I'm going to wait the five years to declare her dead. I think it would be easier for the kids." He didn't like to talk about Eden, but he knew Dylan meant well. To avoid further conversation on the subject, he grabbed the door handle. "To save you from the throngs of your admirers, I'm going to get the kids."

"Hey, I didn't mean to bring down the mood. I just want better for you, man. It's been too long."

Vann nodded. "No harm done. Let me get the kids. Then we can celebrate your return to the Windy City in high style."

"Oh please, not Showbiz Pizza," Dylan moaned.

"Of course not. We're going to Dave and Buster's."

Ivy League stuffy, Dylan was a snob through and through. "I hate that fuc —"

He slammed the truck's door on his friend's complaints and took a spot in the patch of dried grass uncovered from the freshly melting snow.

With his Starbucks Grande latte in hand, he hoped none of the moms in his kid's class noticed him.

"Hi there, stranger! We haven't seen you in forever."

Crap! Fighting his instinct to run, he gave the yoga mom a lame smile and tried to place the peppy woman's face. At six foot two, he was nearly a foot taller than her. He had to outweigh her by at least seventy-five pounds.

"I'm uh…busy. Work." He choked on his coffee drink when she slugged him on the arm.

"Where have you being hiding, you silly goose?"

Head of his own company, and he couldn't believe one PTA mom made him this nervous. He attributed his uneasiness to the manic gleam that shone in her eyes every time they spoke.

After the first week of preschool, Vann had realized single moms were natural predators and he didn't stand a chance against them. From that point on, Marta'd had to pick up the kids. Unfortunately her chipped tooth had forced him out into the wild today. To say he was guarded was an understatement.

"We need a strong, strapping fella like yourself for the spring pageant."

"Well, my schedule is kind of full —"

"I won't take no for an answer," the aggressive woman pushed. "We're meeting at Mary's at four p.m." She gestured at a group of moms who waved back. "Why don't you join us?"

"I, uh… Oh! Hey, there's the boys! I'll see what I can do."

"You know where to find me," she hollered at his back before he could put a good distance between them.

A perky little blonde he had never seen before walked between his kids, holding their hands.

"Are you the twins' dad? I'm Tess, but the kids call me Ms. Tess."

Last Vann knew, the boys' teacher hadn't been this young or cute. It didn't pay to dodge the PTA, he figured. "What happened to Ms. Lori?"

"Her mother had a nasty fall. I'm here until she gets back."

"That's too bad."

Tess smiled sweetly at him as the silence turned awkward. Vann had been alone for some time and he didn't want to get categorized as one of those pervy dads. However, the tips of her nipples pushing against the fabric of her sweater were hard not to notice.

"So…uh, nice meeting you."

"Huh? Oh!" A flush of red crept up her neck. "Sorry. I wanted to tell you that Miles got upset in class today."

"Are you all right, buddy?" He glanced down at his shy twin, but the kid wouldn't look up from his little boots.

"Yeah, I don't know what happened. The class was sharing what their parents did for a living. It was so cute. Louis said you were a green giant." Tess touched his arm with a laugh. "And then when it was time for Miles to talk about his mom, he started to cry."

Vann felt bad. The more sensitive of his two kids, Miles always had a hard time with the no-mom thing.

"My company finds the funding for green start-ups." He tried to clarify the interworking of his three year old's mind. "And my wife is out of the picture." Used to questions about Eden, Vann kept his answer short.

No one wanted to hear that one day she'd taken the boys to the doctor with the nanny but she'd never come back, which was the new version of Dad went out for cigarettes.

Tess' smile slipped into that familiar expression of pity he'd come to expect, but her recovery was better than most. "Well, I certainly didn't think you were a giant, and your job explains the…" She nodded toward his clothes before her words quickly died in her throat. "Oh God! I'm sorry." When she covered her mouth, her blonde hair swung back and forth as she shook her head. "I'm such a goof."

"It's okay." He laughed at her reaction to his worn jeans, plaid shirt and vest. "My job mostly entails places with lots of dirt then coming home to roll around with two three-year-olds." He shrugged. "A suit doesn't make much sense."

"You're right. You're right and I'm sorry."

"No harm done." He laughed again, amused by her embarrassment.

"Hey, Dad," Louis said, interrupting them, "can we go?"

"Sure, sure."

"Well, I have to get back before the head hens scratch my eyes out."

Vann took a glimpse over his shoulder. The mom herd quickly turned away, pretending to be in a deep conversation.

"Single dad with all his teeth… Throw in a horn and just call me a unicorn," he joked. "Besides, you should probably get in there before you get any colder."

Tess followed his eyes down her sweater. The tinkle of her laughter told him she wasn't offended by his observation. "No wonder they're shooting daggers at me," she hiccupped. Vann found her innocence refreshing.

"I want you to take care, Miles," she told the three year old, patting the little boy's arm. "It was nice meeting you, Mr. Morgan." She opened the door and shyly smiled at him over her shoulder.

"Vann," he corrected her. "Call me Vann."

"Okay." She giggled once more before she went inside the school.

Vann guided them through the thick group of older kids who searched for their rides home. "So what do you guys think of your new teacher?"

"I like her," Louis told him. "You should ask her to come over to play."

"Miles?"

His only reply was a shrug. Vann wasn't sure how to interpret that. His older twin could be closed off more times than not.

"Let's go home and watch a movie." Vann ruffled Louis' curly head of hair. "Unless Miles is too upset?"

"I'm okay…"

"Me too," Louis said.

"Great, that means were all okay," he told his boys.

Home of Erotic Romance

Sign up for our newsletter and find out about all our romance book releases, eBook sales and promotions, sneak peeks and FREE romance books!

About the Author

Amber Malloy dreamed of being a double agent but couldn't pass the psyche evaluation. Crushed by despair that she couldn't legally shoot things, Amber pursued her second career choice as pastry chef. When she's not writing or whipping up a mean Snickers Cheesecake, she occasionally spies on her sommelier. Amber is convinced he's faking his French accent.

Amber loves to hear from readers. You can find her contact information, website details and author profile page at https://www.totallybound.com

www.ingramcontent.com/pod-product-compliance
Lightning Source LLC
Chambersburg PA
CBHW032023240626
47154CB00003B/760